序　言

　　學英語只要敢說，很快就能夠跟老外對話，這是不可否認的。但是大部分敢說的人都抱著發音馬馬虎虎，差不多就好的心理，因此終究只能說一些老外勉強聽得懂的話，難怪老外常常要皺眉頭問" Pardon？"「KK音標發音秘訣」不僅能幫助您彌補這項美中不足，更能幫助因為發音不正確而不敢開口的人，突破心理障礙。

　　本書根據國人特殊的發音背景和條件，精心編成，最適合國人初學或矯正使用。並以各種嘴形圖片配合，告訴您英語發音的六大秘訣：

- 如何以國人的習慣，發正確的KK音標
- 一般人感到最難發的音標怎麼發
- 如何區分最混淆的音標
- 如何用連音把話說得流利自然
- 如何把握句子的抑揚頓挫
- 說英語的時候應在什麼地方停頓

從單音到全句的唸法，每一環都不容忽視，才能真正說好英語。

　　本書製有錄音帶，由中美發音老師聯合錄製，發音清晰正確。書和卡帶配合使用，短期內就有意想不到的學習效果，讓您在任何場合都能放膽說出流利悅耳的英語！

　　審慎嚴謹是我們一貫的原則。但些微疏漏恐仍難免，尚祈各方先進惠予賜教。

編者　謹識

　　90％以上的國人，都把 **Thank you**. 唸成 **Sank you**. **mouth** 唸成 **mouse**。雖然自己唸的時候不覺得，老外聽起來却很刺耳，有時候還會鬧笑話。

　　其實 **th** 的發音 /θ/ /ð/，把舌頭伸出即可，非常簡單。一般人之所以唸錯，只因為沒有好的啓蒙老師，所以一錯再錯。

　　從翻開本書的第一頁起，您將永遠不再唸錯。

目　　錄

LESSON 4

LESSON 5

LESSON 6

LESSON 7

LESSON 8

LESSON 12

LESSON 13

LESSON 14

LESSON 19

LESSON 20

LESSON 21

LESSON 22

音標總表

一、母音部份

音標	範　　　例
/ i /	beat〔bit〕, tea〔ti〕
/ ɪ /	sit〔sɪt〕, pig〔pɪg〕
/ e /	day〔de〕, save〔sev〕
/ ɛ /	pen〔pɛn〕, leg〔lɛg〕
/ æ /	cat〔kæt〕, hat〔hæt〕
/ ɑ /	god〔gɑd〕, car〔kɑr〕
/ ʌ /	cut〔kʌt〕, but〔bʌt〕
/ ə /	above〔ə'bʌv〕, capable〔'kepəbl̩〕
/ ɚ /	butter〔'bʌtɚ〕, letter〔'lɛtɚ〕
/ ɝ /	girl〔gɝl〕, bird〔bɝd〕
/ ɔ /	dog〔dɔg〕, ball〔bɔl〕
/ o /	know〔no〕, no〔no〕
/ ʊ /	book〔bʊk〕, good〔gʊd〕
/ u /	shoe〔ʃu〕, two〔tu〕
/ aɪ /	high〔haɪ〕, buy〔baɪ〕
/ aʊ /	round〔raʊnd〕, out〔aʊt〕
/ ɔɪ /	boy〔bɔɪ〕, coin〔kɔɪn〕

二、子音部份

音標	範　　例
/ p /	pen〔pɛn〕, paper〔'pepɚ〕
/ b /	bus〔bʌs〕, back〔bæk〕
/ t /	ten〔tɛn〕, table〔'tebḷ〕
/ d /	desk〔dɛsk〕, do〔du〕
/ k /	key〔ki〕, cup〔kʌp〕
/ g /	get〔gɛt〕, go〔go〕
/ f /	feel〔fil〕, fat〔fæt〕
/ v /	very〔'vɛrɪ〕, over〔'ovɚ〕
/ s /	some〔sʌm〕, stone〔ston〕
/ z /	zoo〔zu〕, season〔'sizṇ〕
/ θ /	thin〔θɪn〕, thank〔θæŋk〕
/ ð /	they〔ðe〕, then〔ðɛn〕
/ ʃ /	she〔ʃi〕, sure〔ʃʊr〕
/ ʒ /	decision〔dɪ'sɪʒən〕, usual〔'juʒʊəl〕
/ tʃ /	church〔tʃɝtʃ〕, chair〔tʃɛr〕
/ dʒ /	gentle〔'dʒɛntḷ〕, just〔dʒʌst〕
/ m /	miss〔mɪs〕, man〔mæn〕
/ n /	nine〔naɪn〕, note〔not〕
/ ŋ /	sing〔sɪŋ〕, bank〔bæŋk〕
/ h /	hot〔hɑt〕, him〔hɪm〕
/ l /	long〔lɔŋ〕, love〔lʌv〕
/ r /	room〔rum〕, rose〔roz〕
/ w /	well〔wɛl〕, wish〔wɪʃ〕
/ j /	yes〔jɛs〕, year〔jɪr〕

發音器官位置圖

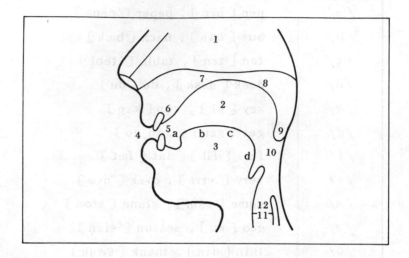

1. 鼻腔　　2. 口腔　　3. 舌（a.舌尖　b.舌前　c.舌中　d.舌根）
4. 唇　　　5. 齒　　　6. 齒齦　　7. 硬顎　　　8. 軟顎
9. 小舌　　10. 咽喉　　11. 聲門　　12. 聲帶

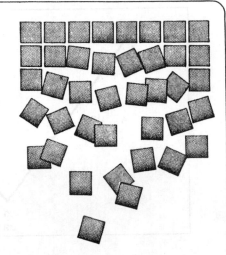

INTRODUCTORY
PRACTICES

介紹英語中的母音系統、子音系統，
但目的不在精通這些音標，而在熟悉
課文中將涵蓋的主要問題。

A ① 五個簡易的母音以及母音位置圖

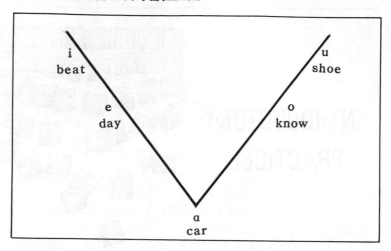

　　這五個母音發音比較容易，是因爲他們跟國語的發音比較相似。然而，也不完全相同，因爲我們發這些音時，通常嘴唇與舌頭移動得更多。請反覆唸下列母音：

$$/ \, i - e - \alpha - o - u \, /$$

　　注意發這些音時的嘴型。發 / i / 時，嘴呈微笑狀；發 / e / 時，嘴半開；發 / α / 時，嘴大開；發 / o / 時，嘴型是圓的，像字母 o；發 / u / 時，雙唇緊合成圓形，並微微突出。請反覆唸下列這五個音：

$$/ \, i - e - \alpha - o - u \, /$$

　　試著去感覺發這些音時，舌頭最高點的位置。發 / i / 時，舌頭最高點在口腔的 " 高前部 "；發 / e / 時是 " 中前部 "；發 / α / 時是 " 低中部 "；發 / o / 時是 " 中後部 "；發 / u / 則在 " 高後部 "。再重覆一次：

$$/ \, i - e - \alpha - o - u \, /$$

A ② 介紹其餘的母音

　　下圖是完整的母音表，除了上述的五個母音外，還有其餘九個母音 / ɪ, æ, ʌ, ə, ɚ, ɝ, ɔ, ʊ /。練習母音有一個很好的方法，就是**把母音插入子音中練習**。請反覆讀下列單字：

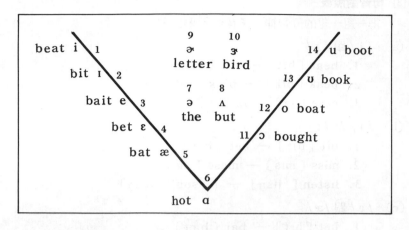

1. [bit] = beat
2. [bɪt] = bit
3. [bet] = bait
4. [bɛt] = bet
5. [bæt] = bat
6. [hɑt] = hot
7. [bʌt] = but

8. [ðə] = the
9. ['lɛtɚ] = letter
10. [bɝt] = Bert（男孩名）
11. [bɔt] = bought
12. [bot] = boat
13. [bʊk] = book
14. [but] = boot

另外尚有三個雙母音無法在圖表中表示：

buy [baɪ] 中的 / aɪ /
now [naʊ] 中的 / aʊ /
boy [bɔɪ] 中的 / ɔɪ /

這些雙母音也很容易發。發 / aɪ / 時，舌頭從 / ɑ / 大約移至 / ɪ / 的位置；發 / ɔɪ / 時，舌頭從 / ɔ / 移至 / ɪ / 的位置；發 / aʊ / 時，舌頭從 / ɑ / 移至 / ʊ / 的位置，但是要記住，發雙母音時，**兩個音之間不可間斷**，要連在一起發音。請反覆唸下面這個句子：

Buy　now　my　boy.
/aɪ/　/aʊ/　/aɪ/　/ɔɪ/

A ③ 母音對照表

把一組一組的母音插入子音中對照練習：

(a) / i / 跟 / ɪ /
1. beat〔bit〕— bit〔bɪt〕
2. peak〔pik〕— pick〔pɪk〕
3. ease〔iz〕— is〔ɪz〕

(b) / ɪ / 跟 / ɛ /
1. bit〔bɪt〕— bet〔bɛt〕
2. miss〔mɪs〕— mess〔mɛs〕
3. listen〔'lɪsn̩〕— lesson〔'lɛsn̩〕

(c) / ɛ / 跟 / æ /
1. bet〔bɛt〕— bat〔bæt〕
2. guess〔gɛs〕— gas〔gæs〕
3. send〔sɛnd〕— sand〔sænd〕

(d) / æ / 跟 / ɑ /
1. sack〔sæk〕— sock〔sɑk〕
2. pat〔pæt〕— pot〔pɑt〕
3. cap〔kæp〕— cop〔kɑp〕

(e) / ɑ / 跟 / ʌ /
1. cop〔kɑp〕— cup〔kʌp〕
2. dock〔dɑk〕— duck〔dʌk〕
3. hot〔hɑt〕— hut〔hʌt〕

(f) / ɑ / 跟 / ɔ /
1. cot〔kɑt〕— caught〔kɔt〕
2. tock〔tɑk〕— talk〔tɔk〕
3. sod〔sɑd〕— sawed〔sɔd〕

(g) / ɔ / 跟 / o /
1. chalk〔tʃɔk〕— choke〔tʃok〕
2. ball〔bɔl〕— bowl〔bol〕
3. bought〔bɔt〕— boat〔bot〕

（h）/ʊ/ 跟 /u/

    1. look〔lʊk〕— Luke〔luk〕

    2. pull〔pʊl〕— pool〔pul〕

    3. soot〔sʊt〕— suit〔sut〕

（i）/ʊ/ 跟 /ʌ/

    1. look〔lʊk〕— luck〔lʌk〕

    2. put〔pʊt〕— putt〔pʌt〕

    3. could〔kʊd〕— cud〔kʌd〕

B① 子音

對英語中主要的子音問題，這裏先做簡單的介紹，以後的課文中，還會提供充份的練習。

首先，我們先介紹子音，有些子音以字母表示，有些則以特別的符號表示。

以字母表達的子音如下：

1. / f / 如 *f*ine, rou*gh*, *ph*one
2. / h / 如 *h*ome, *h*ot, *wh*o
3. / r / 如 *r*ight, *wr*ong, hea*r*
4. / l / 如 *l*ight, *l*ong, hea*l*
5. / n / 如 pe*n*, ca*n*, spoo*n*
6. / s / 如 i*ce*, mi*ss*, *c*ity
7. / z / 如 *Z*ero, doe*s*, pau*s*e
8. / v / 如 *v*ery, ha*v*e, ne*v*er
9. / w / 如 *o*ne, *w*ould, lang*u*age
10. / j / 如 *y*et, *y*awn, *y*oung

以特別符號表達的子音如下：

11. / ʃ / 如 *sh*e, fi*sh*, na*ti*on, ma*ch*ine, o*c*ean
12. / ʒ / 如 u*s*ually, mea*s*ure, lei*s*ure
13. / tʃ / 如 *ch*urch, wa*tch*, fu*t*ure
14. / dʒ / 如 *j*ud*g*e, *G*eor*g*e, a*g*e, pi*g*eon
15. / θ / 如 *th*ink, mou*th*, tee*th*
16. / ð / 如 *th*is, *th*en, fa*th*er, o*th*er, brea*the*
17. / ŋ / 如 si*ng*, ba*n*k, fi*ng*er, E*ng*lish, eati*ng*

B② 子音的基本練習

在下列簡短的練習中，仔細揣摩正確的發音，並反覆練習：

(a) / s / 跟 / z /

1. ice — eyes 　　〔aɪs〕—〔aɪz〕
2. peace — peas 　〔pis〕—〔piz〕
3. bus — buzz 　　〔bʌs〕—〔bʌz〕

(b) / s / 跟 / ʃ /
    1. see 〔 si 〕 — she 〔 ʃi 〕
    2. so 〔 so 〕 — show 〔 ʃo 〕
    3. sue 〔 su 〕 — shoe 〔 ʃu 〕

(c) / s / 跟 / θ /
    1. sick 〔 sɪk 〕 — thick 〔 θɪk 〕
    2. face 〔 fes 〕 — faith 〔 feθ 〕
    3. mouse 〔 maʊs 〕 — mouth 〔 maʊθ 〕

(d) / h / 跟 / f /
    1. heat 〔 hit 〕 — feet 〔 fit 〕
    2. home 〔 hom 〕 — foam 〔 fom 〕
    3. hare 〔 hɛr 〕 — fare 〔 fɛr 〕

(e) / b / 跟 / v /
    1. best 〔 bɛst 〕 — vest 〔 vɛst 〕
    2. boat 〔 bot 〕 — vote 〔 vot 〕
    3. B 〔 bi 〕 — V 〔 vi 〕

(f) / n / 跟 / ŋ /
    1. sin 〔 sɪn 〕 — sing 〔 sɪŋ 〕
    2. ran 〔 ræn 〕 — rang 〔 ræŋ 〕
    3. sun 〔 sʌn 〕 — sung 〔 sʌŋ 〕

(g) / r / 跟 / l /
    1. read 〔 rid 〕 — lead 〔 lid 〕
    2. right 〔 raɪt 〕 — light 〔 laɪt 〕
    3. road 〔 rod 〕 — load 〔 lod 〕

(h) / tʃ / 跟 / dʒ /
    1. cheap 〔 tʃip 〕 — jeep 〔 dʒip 〕
    2. H 〔 etʃ 〕 — age 〔 edʒ 〕
    3. choke 〔 tʃok 〕 — joke 〔 dʒok 〕

(i) / z / 跟 / ð /
    1. Zen 〔 zɛn 〕 — then 〔 ðɛn 〕
    2. breeze 〔 briz 〕 — breathe 〔 brið 〕

（j）/ j / 跟 / i /，/ ɪ /，/ ɛ /

    1. east〔ist〕— yeast〔jist〕

    2. ear〔ɪr〕— year〔jɪr〕

    3. N〔ɛn〕— yen〔jɛn〕

（k）/ w / 的發音

    1. / wi — we — wɑ — wo — wu /

    2. wood〔wʊd〕

    3. woman〔'wʊmən〕

（l）/ ʒ / 的發音

    1. measure〔'mɛʒɚ〕

    2. usually〔'juʒʊəlɪ〕

    3. leisure〔'liʒɚ〕

B③ 有聲、無聲的概念

    子音可分成有聲子音及無聲子音。發有聲子音時，會振動聲帶，發無聲子音則否。以下列出成對的子音，每一對的主要差別，在於一個是無聲，另一個是有聲。

無聲		有聲
/ p /	. . . .	/ b /
/ t /	. . . .	/ d /
/ k /	. . . .	/ g /
/ tʃ /	. . . .	/ dʒ /
/ s /	. . . .	/ z /
/ ʃ /	. . . .	/ ʒ /
/ θ /	. . . .	/ ð /
/ f /	. . . .	/ v /

上表以外的子音皆無法成對，其中無聲子音還有 / h /，有聲子音還有 /m/，/n/，/ŋ/，/ l /，/ r /，/w/，/ j / 等。

B④　有聲、無聲的感覺

用手遮住耳朵，快速地讀 / p / ，不加任何母音：

/ p － p － p － p － p － p － p － p － p － p /

然後，同樣地再試：

/ b － b － b － b － b － b － b － b － b － b /

你聽到 / b / 的聲音會比 / p / 強，因爲 / p / 是無聲，而 / b / 是有聲。同樣再試 / t /、/ d / 以及 / k /、/ g / 。/ d / 比 / t / 強，而 / g / 又比 / k / 強，因爲有聲子音 / d /、/ g / 是無聲子音 / t /、/ k / 出聲後的結果。

重點提示：以上不是字母 P, B, T 等的練習，而是這些字母所代表音標的練習。

～～～～　**Tongue Trippers 繞口令**　～～～～

PETER Piper picked a peck of pickled pepper ;
A Peck of pickled pepper Peter Piper picked.
If Peter Piper picked a peck of pickled pepper,
Where's the peck of pickled pepper Peter Piper
　picked ?

風笛手彼得偸拿了一配克的醃胡椒；
一配克的醃胡椒風笛手彼得偸拿了。
如果風笛手彼得偸拿了一配克的醃胡椒，
這一配克的醃胡椒風笛手彼得偸拿的在哪裏？

piper〔ˈpaɪpɚ〕*n.* 風笛手　　pick〔pɪk〕*v.* 盜竊；挑選
peck〔pɛk〕*n.* 配克（度量單位，英國合 9.092 公升；美國合 8.81 公升）
pickle〔ˈpɪkl̩〕*n., v.* 醃製（物）　　pepper〔ˈpɛpɚ〕*n.* 胡椒

≈≈≈ ≪ **Coffee Break** ≫ ≈≈≈

What would Neptune say if the sea dried up ?

→ *I haven't a notion.*

　如果海枯了，海神會怎麼說？

→我沒有意見。

✦為什麼海枯了以後，海神會說 I haven't a notion（意見）.呢？請你從發音上去想，海神是不是話中有話，想和你玩個文字遊戲，開個玩笑？再唸一唸海神說的：I haven't a notion. 你是不是發現了什麼，足以令你會心一笑，或甚至開懷大笑的？

　　其實海神是說：I haven't *an ocean.*

　　a notion〔ə'noʃən〕和 an ocean〔ən'oʃən〕唸起來是不是一樣？請你再多唸幾次看看。

LESSON 1

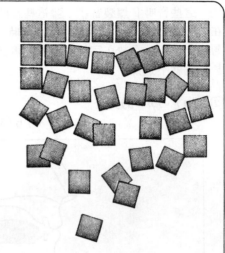

本課介紹所有的爆裂音（/p/，/t/，/k/，/b/，/d/，/g/）的發音方法及部位。

1① /p/、/b/、/t/、/d/、/k/、/g/ 的發音

這些音叫「爆裂音」，發這些音時氣流會短暫停止，如：發 /p/ 時在嘴唇處；發 /t/ 在舌尖碰上齒齦時；發 /k/ 舌頭抵軟顎時，氣流皆短暫停止。這些音放在字首，發音時得送氣出來（即爆發一股氣流），若置於字尾就不送氣。

1② /p/、/b/ 的發音

發 /p/、/b/ 時的位置圖

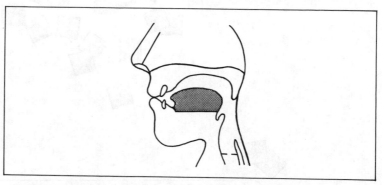

/p/ 和 /b/ 都是用雙唇發的爆裂音。發音時雙唇緊閉，氣流突破雙唇外洩，/p/ 是無聲子音，不須振動聲帶，/b/ 是有聲子音，須振動聲帶。

發字首 /p/ 時所發出的氣流

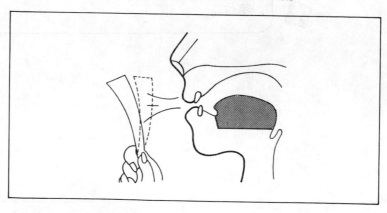

參照上圖，拿一張薄紙放在嘴前，反覆唸：

/ pi — pe — pa — po — pu /

持續練習直到每次你發 /p/ 紙都振動為止。接下來練習字尾的 /p/，發音時得小心，不要在字尾加上一個母音，例如不要發 /pu/。重覆唸幾次：

/ ip — ep — ap — op — up /

持續練習直到能發字尾的 /p/，而不加母音為止。

1③ /t/、/d/ 的發音

發 /t/、/d/ 時的位置圖

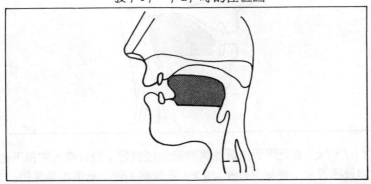

發 /t/、/d/ 時雙唇微開，先用舌尖抵上齒齦，再稍微用力彈開，使氣流外洩。/t/ 是無聲子音，不須振動聲帶，/d/ 是有聲子音，須振動聲帶。

發字首 /t/ 送氣的情形

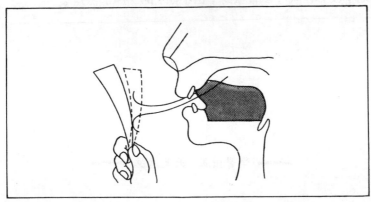

　　依照上圖，拿一張紙放在嘴前，重複唸：
　　　　　　/ ti － te － tɑ － to － tu /
持續練習直到每次你發 / t / ，紙都振動為止。

1 ④ / k / 、/ g / 的發音

發 / k / 、/ g / 時的位置圖

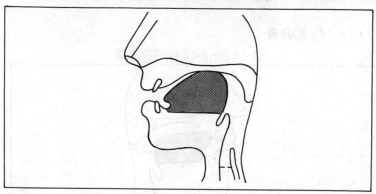

　　/ k / 、/ g / 都是用舌後抵住軟顎發的爆裂音。發音時舌尖抵下齒齦，稍用力放開舌尖，使氣流外洩。/ k / 是無聲子音，不須振動聲帶，　/ g / 是有聲子音，須振動聲帶。

　　依照上圖，拿一張薄紙放在嘴前，重複唸：
　　　　　　/ ki － ke － kɑ － ko － ku /
同樣地，發 / k / 時，紙會振動，但不如 / p / 、/ t / 激烈。

•••••••••• 學習出版，天天進步 ••••••••••

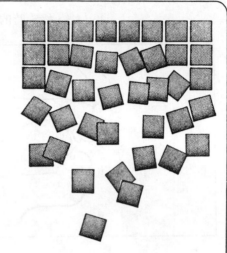

LESSON 2

本課先介紹摩擦音 /s/, /z/ 的發音法
, 以及不定冠詞 a [ə] 及句子的節奏
。然後再討論複數的形成。

2 ① / s /、/ z / 的發音

發 / s /、/ z / 時的位置圖

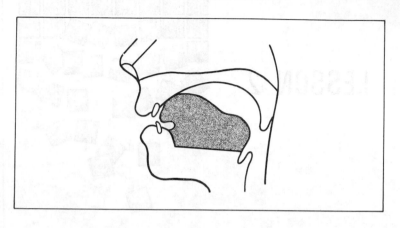

　　/ s /、/ z / 都是摩擦音（發音時氣流被阻擋，但沒有完全切斷）。發音時上下唇微開，用舌尖抵下齒齦，讓氣流摩擦而出。/ s / 是無聲子音，不須振動聲帶；/ z / 是有聲子音，須振動聲帶。

　　讓我們先練習延長後的 / s / 的發音，反覆練習：

　　　　/ s———————— /

　　接下來練習延長有聲的 / z /（振動聲帶）。反覆練習：

　　　　/ z———————— /

　　你可能發現 / s / 比 / z / 容易發，一開始你也許會發〔zʊ〕的延長音，如：

　　　　/ zʊ———————— /

　　可是只要保持舌頭高度，讓舌邊碰到上齒齦，舌頭中間下凹，讓氣流通過，就可以避免誤差。再試試看：

　　　　/ z———————— /

　　還可練習快速從 / s / 換成 / z / ，也能感覺兩者的差別：

　　/ s—— / , / z—— / , / s—— / , / z—— / , / s—— / , / z—— / ……

重點提示：字尾 / z / 正確的發音是英語發音的重點之一，因爲在複數形及第三人稱單數動詞中，它常常出現，一些很常用的字裏也用到了，如 is、was、has、as、these 以及 those，所以很重要。

2 ② 不定冠詞 /ə/ 以及句子的節奏

不定冠詞常發輕音的/ə/，只有特別强調時才發 / e / 。請反覆讀以下生字：

1. a key〔ə ki〕
2. a cake〔ə kek〕
3. a tape〔ə tep〕
4. a pet〔ə pɛt〕
5. a cat〔ə kæt〕
6. a dog〔ə dɔg〕
7. a pot〔ə pɑt〕
8. a coke〔ə kok〕
9. a book〔ə bʊk〕
10. a boot〔ə but〕
11. a pipe〔ə paɪp〕
12. a boy〔ə bɔɪ〕

請記住冠詞的發音，比句中其他音節都要弱得多。通常在每一個英文句裏，都有三種不同的重音。也就是說，英文句子的節奏跟中文相當不同。請比較下列兩句：

中文：這是一隻鉛筆。　　英文：This is a pen-cil.

中文句裏每個字的重音大略相同，可是英文就不一樣了：

主重音以大點表示，落在 *pen-* 上面

次重音以中點表示，落在 *This is* … 上面

輕　音以小點表示，落在 *a* 跟 *-cil* 上面

主重音音節上的字，必須發得很清楚，所以發音時聲音比較大，比較長。屬於輕音的音節，則比較弱，也快多了。大致上，中文句裏每一個字所用的時間都一樣，但在英文句裏，有些音節說得慢，有些音節說得快：

讓我們練習一些簡單句的節奏：

1. I need a desk.
2. I need a coat.
3. I need a tape.
4. I need a pipe.

5. I need a cake.　　　8. I want a key.

6. I want a coke.　　　9. I want a cat.

7. I want a book.　　　10. I want a dog.

2 ③ 有聲子音前的母音比較長

在做 2.1 的練習時，你也許會發現，母音在 /z/ 之前要比在 /s/ 之前長。因為通常母音在有聲子音前要比在無聲子音前長。再舉一些例子：

無　聲	有　聲

〔bit〕= beat　・・・　〔bid〕= bead　（/d/ 之前的 /i/ 比較長）

〔pɪk〕= pick　・・・　〔pɪg〕= pig　（/g/ 之前的 /ɪ/ 比較長）

〔kæp〕= cap　・・・　〔kæb〕= cab　（/b/ 之前的 /æ/ 比較長）

〔etʃ〕= H　　・・・　〔edʒ〕= age　（/dʒ/ 之前的 /e/ 比較長）

2 ④ 複數以及第三人稱單數的形成

依照以下三個原則：

原則一：如果名詞或動詞的字尾是無聲子音，加 s /s/ ：

　　　　　pipe　　→　　pipes〔paɪps〕

　　　　　beat　　→　　beats〔bits〕

　　　　　cake　　→　　cakes〔keks〕

原則二：如果名詞或動詞的字尾是有聲子音，加 s /z/ ：

　　　　　cab　　→　　cabs〔kæbz〕

　　　　　bead　　→　　beads〔bidz〕

　　　　　dog　　→　　dogs〔dɔgz〕

原則三：如果名詞或動詞的字尾是摩擦音（/s/、/z/、/tʃ/、/dʒ/、/ʃ/、/ʒ/）. 加 s 或 es /ɪz/ ：

　　　　　bus　　→　　buses〔'bʌsɪz〕

　　　　　buzz　　→　　buzzes〔'bʌzɪz〕

　　　　　watch　→　　watches〔'watʃɪz〕

　　　　　wish　　→　　wishes〔'wɪʃɪz〕

　　　　　page　　→　　pages〔'pedʒɪz〕

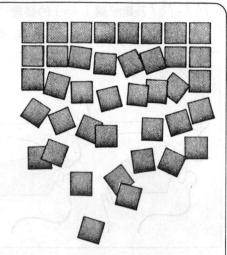

LESSON 3

本課介紹 /θ/, /ð/ 及定冠詞the〔ðə〕
的發音，並區分定冠詞 the 與不定
冠詞 a 發音上的不同，最後還有 be 動
詞縮寫的練習。

3 1 /θ/、/ð/ 及定冠詞〔ðə〕的發音

發 /θ/、/ð/ 時舌頭的位置

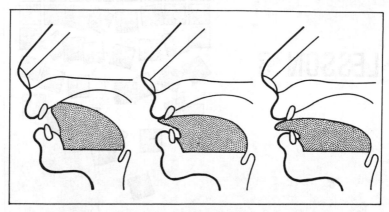

錯誤　　　　　　正確（舌尖伸出一點）　　不妥（舌尖太出來）

上圖顯示兩個 th 可能發的聲音——/θ/ 及 /ð/。兩者都是利用舌尖及牙齒發的摩擦音。發音時舌尖輕抵上齒，再送出氣流。/θ/ 與 /ð/ 之間唯一的差別在 /θ/ 是無聲子音，而 /ð/ 是有聲子音。請反覆練習：

/ ðə — ðə — ðə — ðə — ðə — ðə — ðə — ðə /

3 2 試著體會冠詞 a 以及 the 發音上的不同

冠詞都唸得比較快、比較輕，所以日常對話中，必須訓練自己的聽力，把不同的冠詞區分出來。聽聽下列對比的片語或句子，看你是否能區分出 /ə/ 及 /ðə/：

1. a cake — the cake	2. a seat — the seat
3. a pipe — the pipe	4. a suit — the suit
5. a guide — the guide	6. a boot — the boot
7. a coke — the coke	8. a note — the note
9. a key — the key	10. a date — the date

11. I see a pipe. — I see the pipe.
12. I want a coat. — I want the coat.
13. I want a suit. — I want the suit.

14. I need a key . ─ I need the key .
15. I need a guide . ─ I need the guide .
16. I need a seat . ─ I need the seat .

現在跟著錄音帶重複以上的練習，並用你學過重音不同的讀法帶入句中練習。

以下還有一個聽力測驗，你將聽到一連串成對的句子，裏面有冠詞 /ə/ 或 /ðə/ 或是兩者都有。如果在每一對句子裏，用的冠詞都一樣，就說 " 相同 "；不一樣就說 " 不同 " 。聽的時候先把右邊的答案遮起來。

1. I want the seat . ─ I want the seat . （ 相同 ）
2. I need the key . ─ I need a key . （ 不同 ）
3. I see a pipe . ─ I see a pipe . （ 相同 ）
4. You have the pen . ─ You have a pen . （ 不同 ）
5. He watches a car . ─ He watches the car . （ 不同 ）
6. She likes the doll . ─ She likes the doll . （ 相同 ）

重點提示：注意 want the 中〔 t＋ðə〕以及 need the 中〔 d＋ðə〕的發音。在這種情況下，發〔ðə〕之前先別把爆裂音發出來，也就是說把你的舌頭放在 /ð/ 的位置（ 舌頭抵上排牙齒 ），來發 /t/ 或 /d/ 。以此方式，再重複唸一次：

1. I need the key .   2. I want the key .
3. I need the pipe .   4. I want the pipe .
5. I need the seat .   6. I want the seat .

3 ③ be 動詞的縮寫

be 動詞在說與寫的時候相當不同，我們可能寫：

    I am a student.

但是我們會說：

    I'm a student. 〔 aım ə ˊstjudənt 〕

〔 aım 〕中的 / m / 就是 be 動詞縮寫的發音。其他代名詞也有縮寫的形式，如：

You are   →   You're = [jur] 或 [jʊr]
He is   →   He's   = [hiz] 或 [hɪz]
She is   →   She's   = [ʃiz] 或 [ʃɪz]
It is   →   It's   = [ɪts]
We are   →   We're   = [wir] 或 [wɪr]
They are →   They're = [ðer] 或 [ðɛr]

讓我們以簡單的代換來練習這些縮寫。

反覆練習   I'm busy.   [aɪm ˈbɪzɪ]

you :   You're busy.   [jʊr ˈbɪzɪ]

he :   He's busy.   [hiz ˈbɪzɪ]

nice : He's nice.   [hiz naɪs]

she :   She's nice   [ʃiz naɪs]

it :   It's nice.   [ɪts naɪs]

hot :   It's hot.   [ɪts hɑt]

we :   We're hot.   [wir hɑt]

they : They're hot.   [ðer hɑt]

繼續代換以下的單字：

1. big   2. he   3. you
4. it   5. good   6. she
7. they   8. I   9. we
10. busy   11. he   12. you

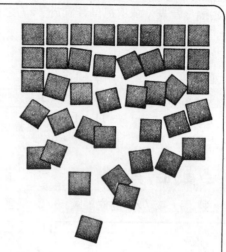

LESSON 4

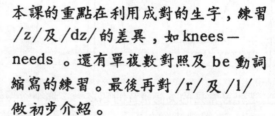

本課的重點在利用成對的生字，練習
/z/ 及 /dz/ 的差異，如 knees —
needs 。還有單複數對照及 be 動詞
縮寫的練習。最後再對 /r/ 及 /l/
做初步介紹。

4 ① 利用母音表練習

對照母音表，依次把母音置於 /z/ 之前，唸的時候特別加重 /z/ 的發音，請反覆練習：

1. 〔iz〕　　　　2. 〔ɪz〕　　　　3. 〔ez〕
4. 〔ɛz〕　　　　5. 〔æz〕　　　　6. 〔ɑz〕
7. 〔ʌz〕　　　　8. 〔ɝz〕　　　　9. 〔ɔz〕
10. 〔oz〕　　　　11. 〔ʊz〕　　　　12. 〔uz〕
13. 〔aɪz〕　　　14. 〔aʊz〕　　　15. 〔ɔɪz〕

4 ② /z/ 與 /dz/ 的對照

發 /s/ 或 /z/ 的位置圖　　　　發 /dz/ 時舌頭的移動

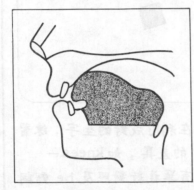 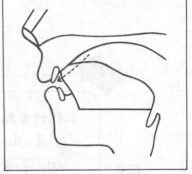

(a) 這是最常見的英語發音問題之一，你不僅得學會 /z/ 及 /dz/ 正確的發音，還得訓練你的耳朵去分辨他們，請注意/dz/中兩個子音要併在一起發。

反覆練習延長後 /z/ 及 /i/ 的發音：

/ i — z — / . . . / i — dz — /

/dz/ 跟 /z/ 最主要的差別在 /dz/ 是一個不連續的音，/z/ 則是連續的。請反覆唸〔id〕，唸的時候不要把 /d/ 的音放開，即保持舌頭在上齒齦的位置：

〔i—d，i—d，i—d，i—d，i—d〕

　　仔細看 / dz / 的圖表。舌頭剛開始在 / d / 的位置，發 / z / 時，有一股氣流從舌中的凹溝流出。這條溝畫不出來，所以用箭頭表示。

　　讓我們練習 knees 跟 needs 中的 / z / 以及 / dz / 。可以比較誇張的方式反覆幾次：

　　　　/ ni － z － , ni － z － , ni － z － / → 〔 niz 〕

　　　　/ ni － d , ni － d / － / ni － d・z － / → 〔 nidz 〕

　　　　/ ni － z － , ni － d・z － , ni － z － , ni － d・z － /→〔 niz, nidz〕

注意：發音時不吐氣的爆裂音，用一個圓點表示，如 / d・/ 。

(b) 觀察差異

　　　　請聽下列的字：

　　　　　　knees － needs　　　　guys － guides

　　　　　　sees － seeds　　　　　cars － cards

　　　　現在請重複唸這些字，並加強 / z / 及 / dz / 的發音：

　　1. needs － knees 〔 ni － d・z , ni － z － 〕→ 〔 nidz 〕,〔 niz 〕

　　2. sees － seeds 　〔 si － z － , si － d・z － 〕→〔 siz 〕,〔 sidz 〕

　　3. guides － guys 〔 ga － ɪd・z － , ga － ɪz － 〕→〔gaɪdz〕,〔 gaɪz 〕

　　4. cars － cards 　〔 kɑ － rz － , kɑ － rd・z － 〕→〔 kɑrz 〕,〔kɑrdz〕

　　　　最後，請練習以下的句子：

　　5. He needs beads. － He needs bees.

　　6. He sees cars. 　　 － He sees cards.

4 ③ / ts / 的發音

　　/ ts / 的發音雖比 / dz / 容易，但是在複數形及第三人稱單數動詞的發音裏，却很重要。/ ts / 的發音相當於 / dz / 的無聲化，所以舌頭的移動完全相同（可以參照先前的圖表）。

　　練習下列的單字，並強調 / ts / 的發音：

　　1. seats 〔 sit・s － 〕　　　　2. sits 　〔 sɪt・s － 〕

　　3. dates 〔 det・s － 〕　　　　4. pots 　〔 pɑt・s － 〕

　　5. notes 〔 not・s － 〕　　　　6. suits 〔 sut・s － 〕

4 ④ 單複數 be 動詞的縮寫

下列有兩對句子：

1. The pipe is new. — The pipes are new.
2. The tie is nice. — The ties are nice.

對話時，這些句子就會縮寫如下：

1. The pipe's new. — The pipes're new.
   〔ðə paɪps nju〕— 〔ðə paɪpsɚ nju〕
2. The tie's nice. — The ties're nice.
   〔ðə taɪz naɪs〕— 〔ðə taɪzɚ naɪs〕

你可以看出，複數名詞與 are 的縮寫只要：

1. 把 / s / 改成 / sɚ / 如〔paɪps〕→〔paɪpsɚ〕
2. 把 / z / 改成 / zɚ / 如〔taɪz〕→〔taɪzɚ〕

因此，只要主詞的字尾是無聲的音（如 / p / ），複數形縮寫就用 / sɚ / 的形式，若是有聲的音（如母音 / aɪ / ），就用 / zɚ / 的形式。現在讓我們來練習 / sɚ / 及 / zɚ / 的發音，記得發 / ɚ / 時，嘴形稍圓，舌頭微向後捲。

/ sɚ , sɚ , sɚ , sɚ , sɚ , sɚ /
/ zɚ , zɚ , zɚ , zɚ , zɚ , zɚ / 強調 / z / 的音

4 ⑤ 單、複數練習
(a) 複數形的句子

1. the book — / sɚ / — new   The books're new.
2. the tape — / sɚ /—easy   The tapes're easy.
3. the seat — / sɚ / — good   The seats're good.
4. the ticket — / sɚ / — cheap   The tickets're cheap.
5. the student — / sɚ / — busy   The students're busy.
6. the coat — / sɚ / — nice   The coats're nice.
7. the summer — / zɚ / — hot   The summers're hot.
8. the teacher — / zɚ / — kind   The teachers're kind.
9. the doctor — / zɚ / — nice   The doctors're nice.

10. the word — /zə/ — easy   The words're easy.

11. the seed — /zə/ — cheap   The seeds're cheap.

12. the guide — /zə/ — busy   The guides're busy.

(b) 聽力練習

錄音帶會隨意選擇左右兩欄中一欄的句子唸出來，請仔細聽以分辨單複數。

單 數	複 數
1. The book's new.	The books're new.
2. The tape's easy.	The tapes're easy.
3. The seat's good.	The seats're good.
4. The ticket's cheap.	The tickets're cheap.
5. The student's busy.	The students're busy.
6. The coat's nice.	The coats're nice.
7. The summer's hot.	The summers're hot.
8. The teacher's kind.	The teachers're kind.
9. The doctor's in.	The doctors're in.
10. The word's easy.	The words're easy.
11. The bird's nice.	The birds're nice.
12. The guide's busy.	The guides're busy.
13. My friend's out.	My friends're out.
14. The suit's new.	The suits're new.

(c) 單複數的轉換（把書闔起來）

錄音帶先唸一次左欄單數的句子，請先跟著唸一遍，然後再自己轉換成複數的句子。

注意 / ts /、/ dz /、/ sə /、/ zə / 的發音。

4⑥ /r/、/l/ 的發音

有些國中學生常將這兩個音混淆，以後的課文裏，還會安排這方面的練習。

(a) / r / 的發音

發 / r / 時的位置圖

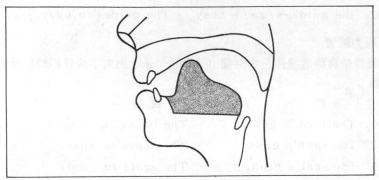

　　/ r / 是流音（氣流從兩側流出），發音時，嘴形稍圓,舌頭向後捲,
（但不要碰到上顎），呼氣較弱，發音時振動聲帶。請反覆練習：

　　　　/ r－i , r－e , r－a , r－o , r－u /
　　　　/ r－i , r－e , r－a , r－o , r－u /
　　　　/ r－i , r－e , r－a , r－o , r－u /

(b) / l / 的發音

發 / l / 時的位置圖

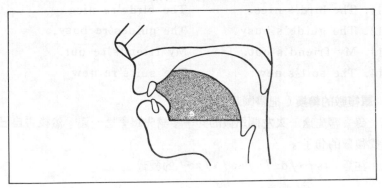

　　/ l / 也是一個流音。發這個音的時候，雙唇微開，用舌前部份抵住
上齒齦，氣流一樣從兩側流出,並振動聲帶。請反覆下面的練習：

　　　　/ l－i , l－e , l－a , l－o , l－u /
　　　　/ l－i , l－e , l－a , l－o , l－u /

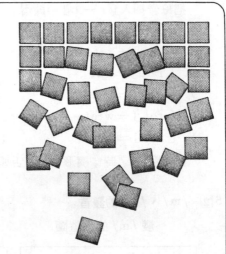

LESSON 5

本課討論有關鼻音的問題。並以 tent
及 sink 作為練習 ten 和 sing 的藍本
，末尾並附加對照練習。

5 ① 利用母音表練習

把母音插入〔r — t〕中練習。

1. 〔rit〕在 greet 中　　　2. 〔rɪt〕= writ
3. 〔ret〕= rate　　　　　　4. 〔rɛt〕在 fret 中
5. 〔ræt〕= rat　　　　　　6. 〔rɑt〕= rot
7. 〔rʌt〕= rut　　　　　　8. 〔rɔt〕= wrought
9. 〔rot〕= wrote　　　　10. 〔rʊt〕（沒有意義）
11. 〔rut〕= root　　　　12. 〔raɪt〕= right

記住發 /r/ 時，嘴形稍圓，舌頭向後捲。

5 ② /m/、/n/ 的發音

發 /m/ 的位置圖　　　　　　發 /n/ 的位置圖

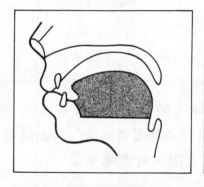 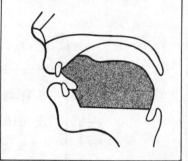

/m/ 是鼻音（氣流通過鼻腔），發音時雙唇閉攏，氣流從鼻腔出來並振動聲帶。

/n/ 也是一個鼻音，發音時用舌前抵住上齒齦，雙唇微開，氣流從鼻腔出來，振動聲帶。

對中國學生來說，字首的 /n/ 發音比較沒有問題，可是在字尾如 ten、man、pin 中的 /n/，就比較容易發錯。然而，在 tent、manned〔mænd〕以及 pinned〔pɪnd〕中的 /n/，又可以發得很正確。這是因為 /t/、/d/ 的舌頭位置與 /n/ 相近。所以，只要先發字尾是 /nt/、/nd/ 的音，再把最後的 /t/、/d/ 去掉，就可以掌握字尾 /n/ 的正確發音了。

先反覆唸 tent 這個字，並加長 / n / 的音：

〔 tɛn — t , tɛn — t , tɛn — t , tɛn — t 〕

現在練習把字尾的 / t / 省略，反覆幾次：

〔 tɛn — t , tɛn — , tɛn 〕

以同樣的方式，練習 end 中 / ɛn / 的部份：

〔 ɛn — d , ɛn — , ɛn 〕

同樣地再練習下列各對單字：

〔 pɪnd 〕	—	〔 pɪn 〕	=	pinned	—	pin
〔 wɪnd 〕	—	〔 wɪn 〕	=	wind	—	win
〔 mɛnd 〕	—	〔 mɛn 〕	=	mend	—	men
〔 mænd 〕	—	〔 mæn 〕	=	manned	—	man
〔 kænd 〕	—	〔 kæn 〕	=	canned	—	can
〔 tɝnd 〕	—	〔 tɝn 〕	=	turned	—	turn
〔 bɝnd 〕	—	〔 bɝn 〕	=	burned	—	burn
〔 wʌnd 〕	—	〔 wʌn 〕	=	………	—	one
〔 gʌnd 〕	—	〔 gʌn 〕	=	gunned	—	gun
〔 sʌnd 〕	—	〔 sʌn 〕	=	sunned	—	sun

接下來，請反覆唸這些字：

1. scene 〔 sin 〕　　　2. sin 〔 sɪn 〕
3. pain 〔 pen 〕　　　4. pen 〔 pɛn 〕
5. pan 〔 pæn 〕　　　6. one 〔 wʌn 〕
7. turn 〔 tɝn 〕　　　8. gone 〔 gɔn 〕
9. bone 〔 bon 〕　　　10. spoon 〔 spun 〕
11. June 〔 dʒun 〕　　12. mine 〔 maɪn 〕
13. down 〔 daʊn 〕　　14. men 〔 mɛn 〕
15. bacon 〔 'bekən 〕

5 ③ /ŋ/ 的發音

發 /ŋ/ 時的位置圖

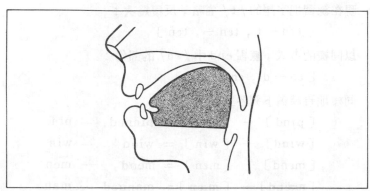

/ŋ/ 也是鼻音，發這個音時，雙唇微開，舌根抵軟顎，讓氣流從鼻腔出來，並振動聲帶。

學習字尾 /ŋ/ 的最佳方法，還是練習發字尾是 /ŋk/ 的字，然後再把 /k/ 去掉。

先反覆唸 sink，並加長 /ŋ/ 的音：

〔sɪŋ—k ，sɪŋ—k ，sɪŋ—k ，sɪŋ—k〕

再練習把字尾的 /k/ 省略，反覆幾次：

〔sɪŋ—k ，sɪŋ— ，sɪŋ〕

以同樣的方式，練習下列各對單字：

〔kɪŋk〕 — 〔kɪŋ〕 = kink — king

〔sæŋk〕 — 〔sæŋ〕 = sank — sang

〔bæŋk〕 — 〔bæŋ〕 = bank — bang

〔sʌŋk〕 — 〔sʌŋ〕 = sunk — sung

〔tʌŋk〕 — 〔tʌŋ〕 = …… — tongue

〔rɔŋk〕 — 〔rɔŋ〕 = …… — wrong

〔lɔŋk〕 — 〔lɔŋ〕 = …… — long

反覆練習下列單字：

1. sing	2. wing	3. rang
4. hang	5. hung	6. young
7. song	8. wrong	9. long
10. singing	11. sinning	12. signing

請練習這些句子：

1. The young king is singing.
2. The king sang the wrong song.

5 ④ 字尾 /n/、/ŋ/ 相互的對照

先聽下列各對單字的差別：

1. sin — sing	2. sing — sin	3. ton — tongue
4. tongue — ton	5. ran — rang	6. rang — ran
7. lawn — long	8. long — lawn	9. sun — sung
10. sung — sun	11. ban — bang	12. bang — ban

再唸一次下列的單字：

sin — sing	win — wing	kin — king
run — rung	lawn — long	ban — bang
ran — rang	ton — tongue	gone — gong

最後請唸這些句子：

1. He ran home.	— He rang home.
2. You shouldn't sin.	— You shouldn't sing.
3. Is that a ton ?	— Is that a tongue ?
4. They want to ban it.	— They want to bang it.

≪**Coffee Break** ≫

If a chicken could talk, what kind of language would it speak ?

→ *Foul language, I'm afraid.*

如果一隻雞能夠說話，它會說哪種語言？

→ 恐怕是髒話。

✦雞如果開口說話，一定是髒話（ Foul language ）嗎？可能是雞話（ Fowl language ）吧！

　　foul〔faul〕*adj.* 骯髒的　　　fowl〔faul〕*n.* 家禽

≪**Coffee Break** ≫

What animal is tiresomely talkative ?

→ *A boar.*

什麼動物異常煩人地愛說話？

→ 雄野豬。

✦特別愛說話煩人的人是 *a bore*〔bor〕，而動物則非 *a boar*〔bor〕（雄野豬）莫屬了。

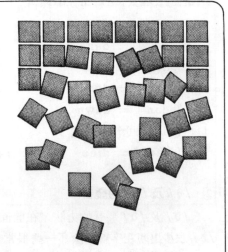

LESSON 6

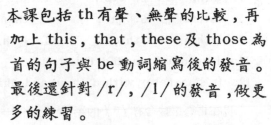

本課包括 th 有聲、無聲的比較，再加上 this, that, these 及 those 為首的句子與 be 動詞縮寫後的發音。最後還針對 /r/, /l/ 的發音,做更多的練習。

6 1 利用母音表練習

把母音插入〔d—n〕中練習。

1. 〔din〕 = dean	2. 〔dɪn〕 = din
3. 〔den〕 = dane	4. 〔dɛn〕 = den
5. 〔dæn〕 = dan	6. 〔dɑn〕 = don
7. 〔dʌn〕 = done	8. 〔dɜn〕（沒有意義）
9. 〔dɔn〕 = dawn	10. 〔don〕 在 don't 中
11. 〔dʊn〕（沒有意義）	12. 〔dun〕 = dune
13. 〔daɪn〕 = dine	14. 〔daʊn〕 = down

6 2 /θ/ 及 /ð/ 的發音

/θ/ 及 /ð/ 發音的方法，在前面的課文裏已稍加討論過。一般來說，/ð/ 很少出現在字首，除了一些很常用的字，如：the、they、this、that、these、those、then、though 之外。其他大部份以 th 起首的字，都是發無聲的 /θ/，如 thin、thick、think、thing 等。

反覆唸以下這些發音中有 /θ/ 的字或句子，記得舌尖要碰到上齒。

1. think	2. teeth	3. third	4. mouth
5. thick	6. thin	7. thank you	8. thousand

9. I think it's thick.　　10. I think it's thin.

11. I need a thousand things.

12. It's monster with a thousand thick teeth.

現在再唸這些含有 /ð/ 的字：

1. the	2. they	3. this	4. that
5. these	6. those	7. then	8. though

6 3 this, that, these, those 的練習

這些字與 be 動詞縮寫後的發音非常重要：

(a) **This is a** 的發音

我們可以把這個片語化成音節，反覆唸幾次，剛開始速度先慢一點：

/ ðɪ — sɪ — zə / —— /ˈðɪsɪzə /

然後再練習一些句子：

         This is a book.
  bag   This is a bag.
  word   This is a word.

代換：

1. pen   2. desk   3. stick
4. shirt   5. tie   6. sweater
7. magazine   8. good book   9. nice suit

你也可以嘗試自己造一些句子。

(b) **These are** 的發音

反覆唸 / ði / 跟 / zə / 這兩個音節：

  / ði, ði, ði / —— / zə, zə, zə / —— / ði — zə /

然後再練習下列句子：

         These're books.
  bags   These're bags.
  words These're words.

代換：

1. pens   2. desks   3. sticks
4. shirts   5. ties   6. sweaters
7. magazines   8. good books   9. nice suits

自己嘗試造一些句子練習。

(c) **That's a** 的發音

在這兒 / ts / 的發音很重要，請反覆唸：

  / ðæts, ðæts, ðæts, ðæts /

再練習下列句子：

         That's a boat.
  dog   That's a dog.
  tape   That's a tape.

代換：

1. teacher   2. window   3. ticket

4. picture   5. piano   6. guide

7. bird   8. car   9. card

自己嘗試造一些句子。

(d) **Those are 的發音**

先反覆唸幾次：

/ ðo, ðo, ðo / —— / zɚ, zɚ, zɚ / —— / ðo — zɚ /

再練習下列句子：

Those're boats.

dogs   Those're dogs.

tapes   Those're tapes.

代換：

1. teachers   2. windows   3. tickets

4. pictures   5. pianos   6. guides

7. birds   8. cars   9. cards

自己嘗試造一些句子。

(e) **代換練習**

請反覆唸

	This is a book.
ticket	This is a ticket.
those	Those're tickets.
workers	Those're workers.
bag	That's a bag.
this	This is a bag.
sweaters	These're sweaters.

再練習：

1. stamps   These're stamps.

2. that   That's a stamp.

3. newspapers   Those're newspapers.

4. these   These're newspapers.

5. picture   This is a picture.

6. piano   This is a piano.

7. those   Those're pianos.

8. cats   Those're cats.

9. magazine   That's a magazine.

10. this   This is a magazine.

11. thick book   This is a thick book.

12. these   These're thick books.

13. third basemen   These're third basemen.

14. that   That's a third baseman.

15. big thing   That's a big thing.

16. those   Those're big things.

6 ④ 複習 /r/、/1/ 的發音

/ r / 的位置圖   / 1 / 的位置圖

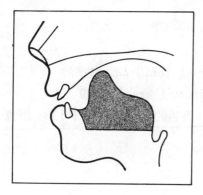 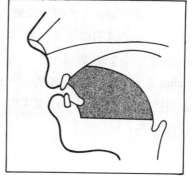

參照上圖複習 / r / 的發音，記住嘴形稍圓，舌頭向後搖

/ ri — re — rɑ — ro — ru /

再練習這些字：

1. read   2. rate   3. red   4. rack

5. rock   6. raw   7. road   8. room

參照上圖複習 / l / 的發音，把舌前部份抵住上齒齦：

/ li — le — lɑ — lo — lu /

再練習這些字：

1. lead	2. late	3. led	4. lack
5. lock	6. law	7. load	8. loom

〜〜〜〜〜〜〜〜〜〜〜〜〜〜〜 **Tongue Trippers 繞口令** 〜〜〜〜〜

My dame hath a lame crane,

My dame hath a crane that is lame

Pray, gentle Jane, let my dame's tame crane

Feed and come home again.

我的貴婦人有一隻跛腳溫順的鶴，

我的貴婦人有一隻鶴是跛腳的

溫柔的珍，請讓我貴婦人溫順的鶴

餵飽並再回家來。

dame〔dem〕*n*. 貴婦人　　lame〔lem〕*adj*. 跛腳的

tame〔tem〕*adj*. 溫順的　　crane〔kren〕*n*. 鶴

gentle〔'dʒɛntḷ〕*adj*. 溫柔的；良善的　　feed〔fid〕*v*. 餵食

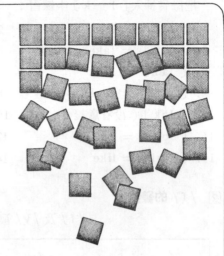

LESSON 7

本課的重點是 /f/ 的發音，在介紹
/f/ 的發音之前一樣有母音的代換練
習，最後再針對名詞單、複形式，做
更多的練習。

7 ① 利用母音表練習

把母音插入〔 l—k 〕中練習：

1. 〔 lik 〕 = leak
2. 〔 lɪk 〕 = lick
3. 〔 lek 〕 = lake
4. 〔 lɛk 〕在 lecture 中
5. 〔 læk 〕 = lack
6. 〔 lɑk 〕= lock
7. 〔 lʌk 〕 = luck
8. 〔 lɝk 〕 = lurk
9. 〔 lɔk 〕（沒有意義）
10. 〔 lok 〕在 cloak 中
11. 〔 lʊk 〕 = look
12. 〔 luk 〕 = Luke
13. 〔 laɪk 〕 = like
14. 〔 laʊk 〕（沒有意義）

7 ② / f / 的發音

/ f / 及 / v / 發音的位置圖

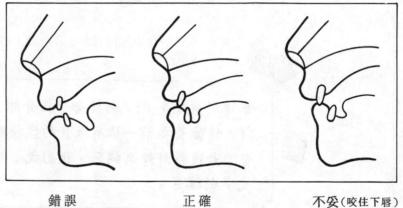

錯誤　　　　　　正確　　　　　　不妥（咬住下唇）

上圖中只有中圖才是 / f /、/ v / 正確的發音位置。/ f /、/ v / 都是摩擦音，發音時把上齒置於下唇上吹氣卽可，不必咬住下唇，只是輕輕的接觸。/ f / 是無聲子音，不必振動聲帶，/ v / 是有聲子音，必須振動聲帶發聲。

先練習一下 / f / 的發音，反覆唸延長的 / f / ：

/ f —— / , / f —— / , / f —— /

氣應該很穩定地從橫隔膜出來，不要吹氣，一吹音就走樣了。再試試看：

$$/ \text{f} — / \, , \, / \text{f} — / \, , \, / \text{f} — /$$

現在練習唸下列的音節：

$$/ \text{fi} — \text{fe} — \text{fa} — \text{fo} — \text{fu} — /$$

也許你覺得發 / fi — fe — fa — / 比 / fo — fu — / 容易，所以再加強練習最後的兩個音節，並延長 / f / 的發音：

$$/ \text{f} — \text{o} \, , \, \text{f} — \text{u} \, , \, \text{f} — \text{o} \, , \, \text{f} — \text{u} /$$

接着練習一些包含 / f / 的單字或句子：

1. feed
2. fit
3. fade
4. fad
5. beef
6. staff
7. laugh
8. rough
9. fork
10. folk
11. foot
12. food
13. few
14. refuse
15. fond
16. roof
17. I like fine food.
18. I eat beef with a fork.
19. Few folks refuse fine food.

7 ③ 單複數練習

（a）受詞及冠詞 / ə / 、/ ðə / 的轉換

I see a student.　　　I see the students.

I see a guide.　　　 I see the guides.

注意：以穩定的節奏及平常說話的速度來做這個練習，a 及 the 都是輕音。

I see a guide.

I see the guides.

繼續以下的練習（單數用 a，複數用 the ）

1. dish
2. seat
3. bed
4. dress
5. boat
6. kid
7. match
8. ticket
9. bird
10. rose
11. cat
12. friend
13. cage
14. coat
15. side
16. nurse
17. suit
18. word
19. bush
20. bat

21. band   22. coach   23. boot   24. speed

25. page   26. kite   27. maid   28. bus

29. pet   30. bud   31. boss   32. student

（b） be 動詞代換的練習

反覆唸	The word's easy.
the words	The words're easy.
long	The words're long.
the lesson	The lesson's long.

繼續以下的練習：

1. difficult	2. the lessons	3. interesting
4. the teacher	5. nice	6. the teacher
7. the suit	8. expensive	9. the tickets
10. the diamond	11. small	12. the diamonds
13. the class	14. late	15. my friends
16. the concert	17. over	18. the classes
19. the program	20. good	21. the programs
22. the guide	23. fine	24. the kids
25. noisy	26. the record	27. cheap
28. the records	29. the ticket	30. the tickets

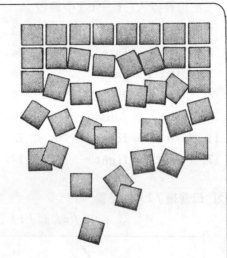

LESSON 8

母音後 /1/ 的發音是本課的主題，並特別討論 will 的縮寫，以及 /ɝl/ 的發音。

8 ① 利用母音表練習

把母音插入〔 f — t 〕中練習。

1. 〔 fit 〕= feet
2. 〔 fɪt 〕= fit
3. 〔 fet 〕= fate
4. 〔 fɛt 〕在 fetter 中
5. 〔 fæt 〕= fat
6. 〔 fɑt 〕（沒有意義）
7. 〔 fʌt 〕（沒有意義）
8. 〔 fɝt 〕在 furtive 中
9. 〔 fɔt 〕= fought
10. 〔 fot 〕在 photo 中
11. 〔 fʊt 〕= foot
12. 〔 fut 〕（沒有意義）
13. 〔 faɪt 〕= fight
14. 〔 faʊt 〕（沒有意義）

8 ② 母音後 / l / 的發音

從 / ə / 到 / l / 舌頭的移動

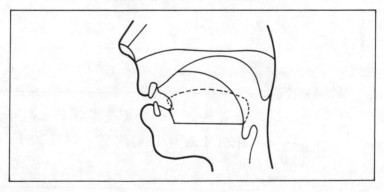

　　讓我們再複習 / l / 的位置圖，並附上與母音 / ə / 的比較，表面上看來，/ l / 可以直接接在任何母音之後，但是我們常常會在母音和 / l / 之間插入 / ə / 的音。例如 peel 實際上是發〔 piəl 〕，但我們通常省略掉 / ə /，把音標寫成〔 pil 〕。所以，如果能正確地發 / əl /，就可以掌握母音後 / l / 的發音。現在讓我們做一些 / əl / 的練習。首先，發 / ə / 時,舌頭完全處於放鬆的狀態，請先重複：

　　　　　　/ ə — ə — ə — ə — ə — ə — ə — ə — ə /

再把 / l / 加上去：

　　　　　　/ lə — əl — ə — əl — ə — əl — ə — əl /

接下來練習把 / əl / 加上去：

〔 fi 〕 → 〔 fiə 〕 → 〔 fiəl 〕 → 〔 fil 〕 = feel

〔 fe 〕 → 〔 feə 〕 → 〔 feəl 〕 → 〔 fel 〕 = fail

〔 kɔ 〕 → 〔 kɔə 〕 → 〔 kɔəl 〕 → 〔 kɔl 〕 = call

〔 ko 〕 → 〔 koə 〕 → 〔 koəl 〕 → 〔 kol 〕 = coal

〔 ku 〕 → 〔 kuə 〕 → 〔 kuəl 〕 → 〔 kul 〕 = cool

〔 maɪ 〕→ 〔 maɪə 〕→ 〔 maɪəl 〕→ 〔 maɪl 〕= mile

8 ③　will 的縮寫

I will　　→ I'll　　= 〔 aɪ-əl 〕
You will　→ You'll　= 〔 ju-əl 〕
He will　 → He'll　 = 〔 hi-əl 〕
We will　 → We'll　 = 〔 wi-əl 〕
They will → They'll = 〔 ðe-əl 〕

練習下列的句子：

1. I'll come tomorrow.　　　2. You'll come tomorrow.

3. He'll come tomorrow.　　 4. We'll come tomorrow.

5. They'll come tomorrow.　 6. Dick'll come tomorrow.

8 ④　/ ɝl / 的發音

從 / ɝ / 到 / l / 舌頭的移動

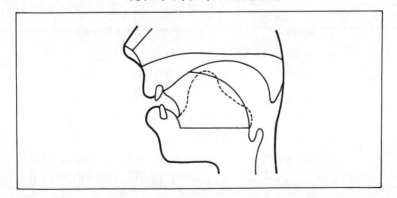

在 girl、pearl、curl 及 world 等字中，都出現 / ɝl / 的組合。讓我們以 girl 為例，先練習 / ɝ / 和 / əl / 這兩個音節：

/ ɝ ─ əl ─ ɝ ─ əl ─ ɝ ─ əl ─ ɝəl ─ ɝəl ─ ɝəl /

發 / ɝ / 時，舌頭、嘴形變動得都很快。首先，舌頭向後捲發 / ɝ / 的音再抵上齒齦發 / l / 的音。發 / ɝl / 的音與發 / əl / 的音道理相同，只要能夠正確地發 / ɝəl / 的音，就可以掌握那些包含 / ɝl / 的生字，例如：

1. 〔 gɝl 〕= girl　　　　　2. 〔 pɝl 〕= pearl
3. 〔 kɝl 〕= curl　　　　　4. 〔 wɝld 〕= world

8 5 母音後 / l / 的練習

(a) 先練習以下的單字：

1. all	2. tall	3. small	4. old
5. cold	6. fold	7. milk	8. silk
9. film	10. child	11. wild	12. spoiled

13. Don't spoil the child.　　14. The old school's cold.
15. Call all the girls.　　　16. The school has a small pool.

(b) 代換

先練習句型　　　　Those girls are small.
　　　　dull　　Those girls are dull.
　　　　old　　Those girls are all old.

再代換：

1. well　　　　Those girls are all well.
2. cool　　　　Those girls are all cool.
3. cold　　　　Those girls are all cold.
4. pale　　　　Those girls are all pale.
5. tall　　　　Those girls are all tall.
6. full　　　　Those girls are all full.
7. beautiful　　Those girls are all beautiful.
8. wonderful　　Those girls are all wonderful.

9. awful　　Those girls are all awful.

10. careful　Those girls are careful.

11. helpful　Those girls are all helpful.

12. skillful　Those girls are all skillful.

(c) 轉換

把形容詞變成副詞：

例如：　careful　She talks carefully.

　　　　good　　She talks well.

再繼續以下的練習：

1. beautiful　She talks beautifully.

2. cold　　　She talks coldly.

3. poor　　　She talks poorly.

4. nice　　　She talks nicely.

5. skillful　She talks skillfully.

6. clear　　　She talks clearly.

7. loud　　　She talks loudly.

8. soft　　　She talks softly.

≈ **Coffee Break** ≈

Why is a book like a hotel ?

→ *Because it has many pages.*

為什麼一本書像旅館一樣？

→ 因為它有很多的書頁。

✦書有很多頁，就像旅館嗎？其實不是這樣的，page 除了當「書頁」的意思，還可以當「旅館的侍者」講，這樣看來，書不是很像旅館嗎？

≈ **Coffee Break** ≈

When is a door not a door ?

→ *When it is ajar.*

門什麼時候就不再是個門？

→ 當它半開時。

✦眞奇怪！門半開時應該還是門呀！爲什麼說當它半開時，就不再是個門呢？ When it is *ajar* 和 When it is *a jar*.（當它是個甕時。）唸起來不是一模一樣嗎？

當它是個甕的時候，當然就不是門了。

ajar〔əˋdʒɑr〕*adj.* 半開的　　jar〔dʒɑr〕*n.* 甕

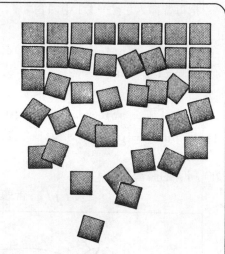

LESSON 9

/j/ 的發音是本課第一個主題，再加上 /i/—/ji/ 的練習。然後複習 /z/—/dz/ 的比較，最後再討論單複數的互換。

9 1 利用母音表練習

把母音插入〔p－1〕中練習。

1. 〔pil〕= peel   2. 〔pɪl〕 = pill

3. 〔pel〕= pale   4. 〔pɛl〕在 pellet 中

5. 〔pæl〕= pal   6. 〔pʌl〕在 pulse 中

7. 〔pɝl〕= pearl   8. 〔pɔl〕= Paul

9. 〔pol〕= pole   10. 〔pʊl〕= pull

11. 〔pul〕= pool   12. 〔paɪl〕= pile

9 2 / j / 的發音

發 / j / 時舌頭的位置

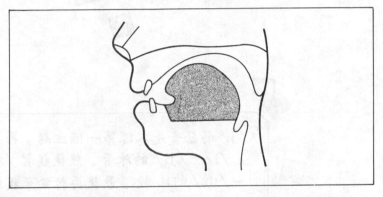

/ j / 是個滑音（氣流不受阻擋），發此音時，舌前部份升向上顎，雙唇扁平，氣流輕輕摩擦而出。

/ ji / 跟 / i / 比較難區分，反覆練習：

/ i － ji － i － ji － i － ji /

再唸以下的單字：

1. ear〔ɪr〕— year〔jɪr〕

2. east〔ist〕— yeast〔jist〕

3. ale〔el〕—〔jel〕

4. S〔ɛs〕— yes〔jɛs〕

最後把上面的單字帶入句中練習：

     1. They make **yeast** in the **east**.

     2. They drink ale at Yale.

     3. I hurt my ear a year ago.

9 ③ 複習 / z / 的發音

/ s / 及 / z / 的位置圖

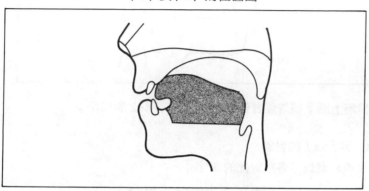

  / z / 是重要的英語發音問題之一，所以必須掌握正確的發音。注意發 / s /、/ z / 時，舌尖向下，讓舌兩邊碰到上齒齦，舌頭中間下凹，使氣流從中通過。首先，先練習 / s / 的發音：

       / s —— / , / s —— /

然後再出聲發延長的 / z / ：

       / z —— / , / z —— /

如果發成 / zʊ / ：

       / zʊ —— /

  那是因爲舌頭的位置不對，在前面加上 / ɑ / 的音，也許可以使舌頭的位置正確，因爲 / ɑ / 是有聲的，對發延長的 / z / 有所幫助。

    / ɑ — z —— / , / ɑ — z —— / , / ɑ — z —— /

9 ④ 複習 / dz / 的發音

/ dz / 的位置圖

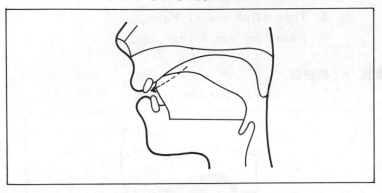

請參照上圖，跟着錄音帶複習第四課，4·2的部份。

9 ⑤ / z / 與 / dz / 的對照

請反覆練習以下各組對比的單字：

1. bees〔biz〕— beeds〔bidz〕
2. sees〔siz〕— seeds〔sidz〕
3. maze〔mez〕— maids〔medz〕
4. size〔saɪz〕— sides〔saɪdz〕
5. guys〔gaɪz〕— guides〔gaɪdz〕
6. rise〔raɪz〕— rides〔raɪdz〕
7. buzz〔bʌz〕— buds〔bʌdz〕
8. burrs〔bɝz〕— birds〔bɝdz〕
9. rose〔roz〕— roads〔rodz〕
10. cars〔kɑrz〕— cards〔kɑrdz〕

9 ⑥ 單複數的變換

我們現在要針對動詞的第三人稱單數及複數變換，做一些練習，例如：

The train stops here.　　　　The trains stop here.

　　這其中包含了 s 的位置（可發 / s / 或 / z / ，依情況而定）從動詞到主詞，或從主詞到動詞的轉移。請快速重複以下的練習，注意單複數變化時，s 位置的移動。

單 數	複 數
1. The boy sees.	The boys see.
2. My sister wants.	My sisters want.
3. My friend knows.	My friends know.
4. The teacher needs.	The teachers need.
5. The bus goes.	The buses go.
6. The student understands.	The students understand.
7. The guide speaks.	The guides speak.
8. The girl repeats.	The girls repeat.

單 數	複 數
1. The train stops here.	The trains stop here.
2. The teacher speaks fast.	The teachers speak fast.
3. The boy watches TV.	The boys watch TV.
4. The guide eats here.	The guides eat here.
5. My friend needs a rest.	My friends need a rest.
6. The student repeats the words.	The students repeat the words.
7. The patient needs medicine.	The patients need medicine.
8. The girl likes the picture.	The giris like the picture.
9. The teacher uses chalk.	The teachers use chalk.
10. My friend lives here.	My friends live here.
11. The car goes fast.	The cars go fast.
12. The ticket costs a lot.	The tickets cost a lot.

```
******* ≪Coffee Break ≫ *********************************
*
*  What is the longest word in the English language?
*  → *Smiles, because there is a mile between its first*
*       *and last letters.*
*
*  英語中最長的字是什麼？
*  → smiles（微笑），因為它的第一個和最後一個字母之間有
*       一哩之長。
*
*********************************************************
```

✦你能想像英文之中最長的字只有六個字母嗎？你一定不相信，對不對？沒有關係，但你能想出頭尾兩個字母之間比一哩（mile）更長的英文字嗎？如果有的話，請你寫下來，好嗎？

　　這兒，我們列了兩個相當長而充滿趣味的英文字

　　　floccinaucinihilipilification （ 29個字母）

　　　anti-Establishmentarian （ 22個字母）

　　是不是很有意思？

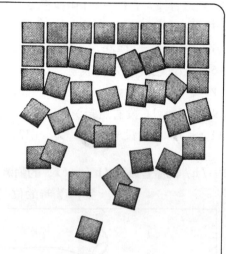

LESSON 10

本課先討論 /h/ 的發音，再跟 /f/ 做對照練習。然後討論 /v/ 的發音，及 /b/ 的對照，最後再加上一些單複數變換的練習。

10 1 利用母音表練習

把母音插入〔f—z〕中練習：

1. 〔fiz〕= fees   2. 〔fɪz〕= fizz
3. 〔fez〕= faze   4. 〔fɛz〕= fez
5. 〔fæz〕（沒有意義）   6. 〔fɑz〕（沒有意義）
7. 〔fʌz〕= fuzz   8. 〔fɝz〕= furs
9. 〔fɔz〕（沒有意義）   10. 〔foz〕= foes
11. 〔fʊz〕（沒有意義）   12. 〔fuz〕（沒有意義）

10 2 / h / 的發音以及 / h / 、 / f / 的對照

發 / h / 時的位置圖

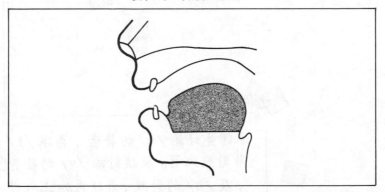

　　/ h / 也是一個摩擦音，發這個音時，口半開，讓氣流通過聲門出來，但是不振動聲帶。

　　英語中 / h / 的音，不如國語強。/ h / 本身沒有很固定的嘴型，會受其後母音的影響，尤其在碰到發音部位比較偏後的母音，如 / o / 、/ u / 時，/ ho / 、/ hu / 容易跟 / fo / 、/ fu / 混淆，必須作一辨別。

　　練習發 / h / 的音，先發母音：

　　　　/ i — e — ɑ — o — u /

　　現在，利用發這些母音的嘴型，把 / h / 的音加上，由慢而快地練習：

　　　　/ hi — he — hɑ — ho — hu /

　　　　He　Hay　Ha　　Ho　WHo

接下來，換上 / f / 的音：

/ fi — fe — fɑ — fo — fu /

然後再對照唸：

/ hi — fi / — / he — fe / — / hɑ — fɑ / — / ho — fo / — / hu — fu /

最後練習以下的生字及句子：

1. her — fur
2. honey — funny
3. halt — fault
4. hold — fold
5. hone — phone
6. home — foam
7. who'd — food
8. who'll — fool
9. Hugh — few
10. That's funny, honey !
11. Please hold the phone.
12. Who's a fool ?
13. Who'd eat that food !
14. Hugh has a phone at home.

10 ③ /v/ 的發音

發 / v / 的位置圖

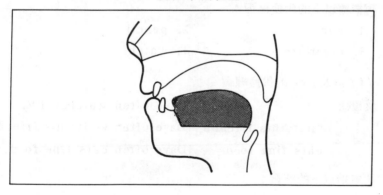

發 / v / 的嘴形與 / f / 完全一樣，唯一的差別在 / v / 必須振動聲帶，而 / f / 則否。然而，發 / v / 時，可能有變成 / b / 的傾向。因此，可以拿一隻鉛筆，抵在上排前齒之前，以防嘴唇閉上，而變成 / b / 的音。

反覆唸

/ vi — ve — vɑ — vo — vu /

再練習以下的單字及句子：

1. TV　　　　2. veil　　　　3. vest　　　　4. value

5. vote　　　6. view　　　7. Dave　　　8. arrive

9. above　　10. ever　　11. never　　12. curve

13. Dave arrived at five.　　14. What a lovely view !

15. Eve never votes.　　16. I've never arrived late.

10 4 /v/ 及 /b/ 的對照

反覆唸以下成對的單字，並體會其中的不同：

1. TB — TV　　　2. best — vest　　　3. berry — very

4. bat — vat　　　5. boat — vote　　　6. robe — rove

10 5 有關 /h/、/f/ 以及 /v/ 的練習

（a）反覆唸　　　　　Who has a pen ?

　　　　　　book　　Who has a book ?

再繼續以下的代換練習：

　　1. car　　　　　　2. pencil

　　3. cigarette　　　　4. watch

（b）/f/ 以及 /v/ 的代換練習

　　反覆唸　　　　　　　　Dave often watches TV.

　　　　　visits his friends　Dave often visits his friends.

　　　　　eats fine food　　Dave often eats fine food.

再繼續以下的練習：

　　1. takes a vacation　　2. visits the office

　　3. never　　　　　　4. phones home

　　5. fixes a fuse　　　6. arrives before five

　　7. behaves like a fool　8. drives a van

10 ⑥ 單複數的練習

請先跟著錄音帶唸左欄單數的例句，然後不看書把複數的句子說出來。

1. The teacher speaks fast.　　The teachers speak fast.

2. The lesson's easy.　　　　The lessons're easy.

3. The student eats at six.　　The students eat at six.

4. The word's difficult.　　　The words're difficult.

5. The guide speaks English.　The guides speak English.

6. The record's expensive.　　The records're expensive.

7. The seat's comfortable.　　The seats're comfortable.

8. The student repeats well.　The students repeat well.

9. The shirt's colorful.　　　The shirts're colorful.

10. The boy needs books.　　The boys need books.

11. The road's long.　　　　The roads're long.

12. The girl needs money.　　The girls need money.

13. My friend lives there.　　My friends live there.

14. The guide's late.　　　　The guides're late.

15. The ticket's cheap.　　　The tickets're cheap.

16. The student practices here.　The students practice here.

17. The artist paints here.　　The artists paint here.

18. The classroom's cold.　　The classrooms're cold.

19. The cost's high.　　　　The costs're high.

20. The patient needs medicine.　The patients need medicine.

************ **Tongue Trippers 繞口令** ***************

BETTY Botter bought some butter.

But, she said, the butter's bitter ;

If I put it in my batter

It will make my batter bitter,

But a bit of better butter,

That would make my batter better.

So she bought a bit of butter

Better than her bitter butter,

And she put it in her batter

And the batter was not bitter

So it was better Betty Botter

Bought a bit of better butter

蓓蒂・勃特買了一些奶油，

但是，她說，奶油是苦的；

如果我把它加進做糕點的麵糊裏

它會使我的麵糊變苦，

只要一點好一點的奶油，

就會使我的麵糊好些。

於是她買了一點奶油

比她的苦味奶油好一點，

她把它放進她的麵糊

麵糊就不苦了。

所以好在蓓蒂・勃特

買了一點好一點的奶油。

butter 〔ˈbʌtɚ〕 *n.* 奶油　　　bitter 〔ˈbɪtɚ〕 *adj.* 苦的

batter 〔ˈbætɚ〕 *n.* 麵粉、蛋、牛奶等用以調製糕點的糊狀物

LESSON 11

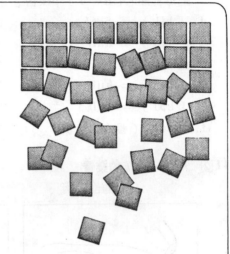

本課先介紹 /ʃ/ 的發音，再跟 /s/ 對照。同時也練習 /ʒ/，/tʃ/，/dʒ/ 這幾個音，最後再集中討論 /s＋ʃ/，/z＋ʒ/，/tʃ＋t 或 d/ 以及 /dʒ＋t 或 d/ 的發音問題。

11 ① 利用母音表練習

把母音插入〔h — l〕中練習。

1. 〔hil〕= heal
2. 〔hɪl〕= hill
3. 〔hel〕= hail
4. 〔hɛl〕= hell
5. 〔hæl〕= hal
6. 〔hɑl〕（沒有意義）
7. 〔hʌl〕= hull
8. 〔hɝl〕= hurl
9. 〔hɔl〕= hall
10. 〔hol〕= hole
11. 〔hʊl〕（沒有意義）
12. 〔hul〕= who'll

11 ② /ʃ/、/ʒ/ 的發音

/ʃ/ 的位置圖	/s/ 的位置圖

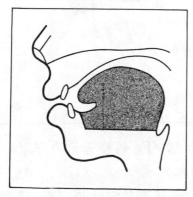 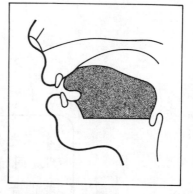

/ʃ/ 是個摩擦音，發這個音時，雙唇微向前突，舌前接近硬顎前部，氣流摩擦而出。/ʒ/ 發音方法跟 /ʃ/ 完全一樣，但是 /ʃ/ 是無聲子音，而 /ʒ/ 是有聲子音。

比較 /ʃ/ 跟 /s/ 的位置圖可以發現，發 /ʃ/ 時舌頭的位置比較偏後，而且嘴形也比較圓，但還是有人會把 see — she，sip — ship 等音混淆在一起。所以，讓我們來做個對照，先練習發延長的 /ʃ/：

/ ʃ —— / ，/ ʃ —— / ，/ ʃ —— /

如果你發得不夠正確，是因為舌頭的位置不對。把舌中再提高點試試看。

接下來練習一些有 /ʃ/ 的字：

1. she　　　2. ship　　　3. shame　　　4. shell
5. shock　　6. shut　　　7. should　　　8. shoe
9. action〔ˊækʃən〕　　10. nation〔ˊneʃən〕
11. ocean〔ˊoʃən〕　　12. machine〔məˊʃin〕
13. wish〔wɪʃ〕　　14. wash〔wɑʃ〕
15. push〔pʊʃ〕

11 ③ /s/跟 /ʃ/ 的對照

先反覆唸這一對單字：

　　　　see — she　（〔si〕—〔ʃi〕）

再練習：

1. seep — sheep　　2. seat — sheet　　3. seen — sheen
4. sees — she's　　5. seed — she'd　　6. sip — ship
7. socks — shocks　8. suit — shoot　　9. sues — shoes

接下來再唸一些有 /s/ 跟 /ʃ/ 的句子：

1. She likes the sea.　　2. She has a machine.
3. She sees the show.　　4. She sees the sea.
5. She sees the machine.　6. She sees the scene.
7. She should buy the suit.　8. She should see the machine.

11 ④ /tʃ/ 跟 /dʒ/ 的發音

發 /tʃ/、/dʒ/ 時舌頭的移動　（……）是開始的位置
（——）是最後的位置

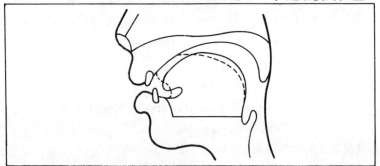

　　/ tʃ /、/ dʒ / 是爆擦音（氣流先被阻擋，然後才釋放）。/ tʃ / 等於 / t＋ʃ / ，是無聲子音。/ dʒ / 等於 / d＋ʒ / ，是有聲子音。

　　重複練習以下的單字，注意發 / tʃ /、/ dʒ / 之前的 / t· /、/ d· / 時，都不要把氣吐出來。

1. cheap　　　　　2. jeep　　　　　3. church

4. judge　　　　　5. rich　　　　　6. ridge

7. pigeon〔ˈpɪdʒən〕　8. language〔ˈlæŋgwɪdʒ〕

11 5　/ z＋ʃ / 的發音

　　如果我們把 does 和 she 分開來唸，發音是〔dʌz〕＋〔ʃi〕，但是合在一塊唸時，發音就改變了。因為〔ʃɪ〕裏面的 / ʃ / ，影響〔dʌz〕中 / z / 的發音，而由 / z / 轉變成 / ʒ / ，所以 does she 便發成 / dʌʒʃi / 。

　　現在讓我們來練習這個音：

〔dʌʒʃi，dʌʒʃi，dʌʒʃi，dʌʒʃi〕

　　同樣的方式，在 Yes, she does. 裏，yes 的 / s / 也轉變成 / ʃ / ，而變成〔jɛʃʃi dʌz〕。

　　以下有一些 Does she …? Yes, she does. 的問答練習，請跟著錄音帶一起唸。

study English

Does she study English ?

Yes, she does.

再繼續以下的代換：

1. play tennis　　　2. watch television　3. like movies

4. go to church　　5. use a dictionary　6. wash the dishes

7. teach German　　8. study languages

接下來再把 usually 加進每一個句子裏：

study English

Does she usually study English ?

Yes, she usually does.

重複以上的代換練習。

11 ⑥　/tʃ/、/dʒ/ 在 /t/、/d/ 之前的發音

　　當一個字的字尾是 /tʃ/ 或 /dʒ/，而其後又跟著一個字首是 /t/ 或 /d/ 的字時，發音可能比較麻煩。請反覆以下的練習，使自己適應這些字的發音，並注意把 /tʃ/、/dʒ/ 跟其後的 /t/、/d/ 分開來唸。

　　1. much ˊtime　　　　　2. much ˊtea
　　3. much ˊdamage　　　4. each ˊdate
　　5. a large ˊdinner　　　6. a large ˊdish
　　7. a large ˊtable　　　　8. a ˊlanguage tape
　　9. a package ˊtour　　　10. a village ˊdance

11 ⑦　/s/ 跟 /ʃ/ 的練習

　　反覆練習以下的問答：

　　　　Does she see the sea？　/ dʌʒʃi· si ðə si /
　　　　Yes, she sees the sea.　/ jɛʃʃi siz ðə si /

　　要把 sees 的 /z/ 唸得很清楚。

≪**Coffee Break**≫

Why is a plum pudding like the ocean？
→ *It's full of currants.*
　爲什麼葡萄干布丁像海洋一樣？
→ 因爲它充滿了葡萄干。

　　✦ currant 是葡萄干，爲什麼充滿了葡萄干的布丁會像海洋一樣呢？別忘了，currant 有一個同音字，就是 *current* 〔ˊkɝənt〕海流。

　　現在知道爲什麼充滿葡萄干的布丁像海洋了吧！

　　plum〔plʌm〕*n.*（做糕餅用的）葡萄乾

≫ ≪Coffee Break≫

What did the zero say to the numbers?

→ *Without you, I'm nothing.*

零對數字說什麼?

→ 沒有你們,我便一文不名。

What did the wall say to the ceiling?

→ *The wall said, " See you at the corner."*

牆對天花板說什麼?

→ 牆說:「轉角見。」

✦聽數字和靜物發表意見,與他們周圍的朋友溝通,也是很有趣的事。

0(零)如果沒有和其他數字連在一起,就永遠是0(nothing);如果跟其他數字連用,作用就很大了,如3之後加一個0就是30了。

牆和天花板相接的地方,就是在角落,所以說「轉角見。」

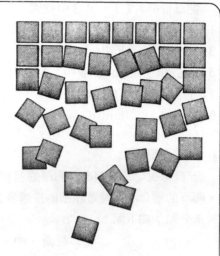

LESSON 12

本課著重於母音的介紹，以及對照練習。最後還比較 /θ/ 與 /s/ 的差異。

12 ① 利用母音表練習

把母音插入〔ʃ－d〕中練習。

1. 〔ʃid〕= she'd
2. 〔ʃɪd〕（沒有意義）
3. 〔ʃed〕= shade
4. 〔ʃɛd〕= shed
5. 〔ʃæd〕在 shadow 中
6. 〔ʃad〕= shod
7. 〔ʃɔd〕（沒有意義）
8. 〔ʃod〕= showed
9. 〔ʃʊd〕= should
10. 〔ʃud〕= shooed

12 ② 母音介紹

一般來說，子音都有其明確的發音位置及方法，然而母音却偏重於口腔、嘴型的變化，比較難詳細地描述發音方法。通常以舌頭位置的高低、前後來分類，如下圖：

（口腔前、中、後部）

嘴型	前	中	後	嘴型
扁	i		u	圓
	ɪ		ʊ	
	e	ɝ	o	
		ɚ		
		ə		
	ɛ	ʌ		
開	æ	ɑ	ɔ	開

（舌頭位置高中低）　高　中　低

練習下列單字，以熟悉這些母音的發音，請跟著錄音帶唸：

/i/	f*ea*st	agr*ee*	br*ie*f	m*ea*n
/ɪ/	bus*y*	pon*y*	s*ie*ve	prett*y*
/e/	br*ea*k	gr*ey*	*ei*ght	r*ei*n
/ɛ/	w*e*st	l*e*tter	*a*ny	p*e*n
/æ/	c*a*rry	*a*sk	th*a*nk	c*a*b
/ɝ/	g*ir*l	n*ur*se	h*ur*t	p*ur*pose
/ɚ/	teach*er*	fig*ure*	tut*or*	fav*or*

/ə/	fam**ou**s	**a**nnoy	**o**pen	**a**ware
/ʌ/	c**o**ver	d**o**ve	b**u**tter	d**u**ll
/ɑ/	h**ea**rt	**a**re	c**a**lm	p**a**rk
/u/	bl**ue**	r**u**le	fr**u**gal	n**oo**n
/ʊ/	g**oo**d	w**o**lf	f**oo**t	b**u**sh
/o/	s**ou**l	**o**dor	b**o**w	h**o**le
/ɔ/	c**o**rd	b**a**ll	t**a**lk	l**o**ng

12 ③ /æ/ 與 /ɛ/ 的比較

(a) 一些包含 /æ/ 的單字

1. **a**bsent   2. **a**ccent   3. **a**pple   4. **a**venue
5. b**a**g   6. b**a**th   7. f**a**mily   8. th**a**t
9. m**a**n   10. c**a**mp   11. d**a**nce   12. h**a**ppy
13. h**a**ve   14. gr**a**duate   15. gr**a**mmar   16. **a**ngry

(b) /æ/ 的代換練習

	That man's dancing.
happy	That man's happy.
having a bath	That man's having a bath.

代換：

1. angry   2. laughing
3. standing   4. packing his bags
5. having a sandwich   6. catching a cab
7. absent from class   8. passing the path
9. having a laugh

(c) 比較

練習以下這兩個重要單字：

man〔mæn〕— men〔mɛn〕

再重覆唸幾次，就可以發現 /æ/ 的舌頭位置比較低，嘴巴比較開。

另外，還得注意 /n/ 的發音（參考第五課）。

繼續以下的對照練習：

1. set ─ sat　　2. head ─ had　　3. pen ─ pan

4. guess ─ gas　5. shell ─ shall　6. left ─ laughed

再練習以下的句子：

1. The men came. ─ The man came.

2. They guessed it. ─ They gassed it.

3. He left quickly. ─ He laughed quickly.

4. We set out.　　 ─ We sat out.

12 ④ / æ / 與 / ɑ / 的比較

/ ɑ / 的舌頭位置比較低，嘴型近於全開，請跟著錄音帶唸：

	/ æ /	/ ɑ /		/ ɑ /	/ æ /
1.	hat	hot	5.	hot	hat
2.	sack	sock	6.	sock	sack
3.	lack	lock	7.	lock	lack
4.	cap	cop	8.	cop	cap

12 ⑤ / ɑ / 與 / ʌ / 的比較

發 / ʌ / 時舌頭完全放鬆，請練習：

	/ ʌ /	/ ɑ /		/ ɑ /	/ ʌ /
1.	nut	not	6.	not	nut
2.	hut	hot	7.	hot	hut
3.	luck	lock	8.	lock	luck
4.	duck	dock	9.	dock	duck
5.	cup	cop	10.	cop	cup

接下來練習 / æ / ─ / ɑ / ─ / ʌ / 的對照：

	/ æ /	/ ɑ /	/ ʌ /
1.	hat	hot	hut
2.	lack	lock	luck
3.	cap	cop	cup

反覆唸以下兩個句子：

1. Pat sat in the hot hut.
   / æ   æ   ɑ   ʌ /

2. The cop with a cup has a cap.
   / ɑ   ʌ   æ   æ /

12 ⑥ /ɔ/ 與 /o/ 的比較

/ o / 的舌頭位置比 / ɔ / 高，嘴型也比較圓，請跟錄音帶練習：

	/ɔ/	/o/		/o/	/ɔ/
1.	bought	boat	5.	boat	bought
2.	chalk	choke	6.	choke	chalk
3.	cost	coast	7.	coast	cost
4.	pause	pose	8.	pose	pause

區分以上這些字也許並不難，但是 / ɔ /、/ o / 之後有 / l / 的音，就比較容易混淆，請跟著唸：

	/ɔ/	/o/		/o/	/ɔ/
1.	call	coal	7.	coal	call
2.	ball	bowl	8.	bowl	ball
3.	fall	foal	9.	foal	fall
4.	tall	toll	10.	toll	tall
5.	bald	bold	11.	bold	bald
6.	called	cold	12.	cold	called

接著練習以下的句子：

1. I called him cold.　　2. I saw the foal fall.
3. All the old men called.　4. The ball is in the bowl.

12 ⑦ /i/ 與 /ɪ/ 的比較

/ i / 的舌頭位置比 / ɪ / 高，發音時口腔肌肉繃得比較緊，嘴型比較扁，請練習以下各組單字，以區分差別所在：

1. beat — bit	2. seek — sick	3. deep — dip
4. ease — is	5. he's — his	6. deed — did
7. bit — beat	8. sick — seek	9. dip — deep
10. is — ease	11. his — he's	12. did — deed

12 ⑧ /ɪ/ 與 /ɛ/ 的比較

/ɪ/ 的舌頭位置比 /ɛ/ 高，兩者都是發音時肌肉比較鬆弛的母音，但 /ɛ/ 的嘴型比 /ɪ/ 開，請比較下列各組單字的不同：

1. bit — bet	2. did — dead	3. Dick — deck
4. miss — mess	5. wrist — rest	6. listen — lesson
7. bet — bit	8. dead — did	9. deck — Dick
10. mess — miss	11. rest — wrist	12. lesson — listen

12 ⑨ /θ/ 與 /s/ 的比較

/s/ 的位置圖   /θ/ 的位置圖

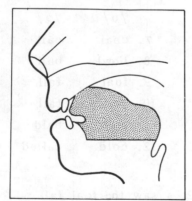 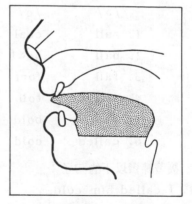

很多人不清楚 /θ/ 和 /s/ 的差異，因而在發音上一視同仁，造成很多的混淆，例如把 think 唸成 sink 等等。讓我們對照著圖表復習一下這兩個音標，以掌握其正確的發音。首先，先反覆唸一些字首是 /θ/ 的字：

1. think	2. thing	3. thought	4. theme
5. thick	6. thumb	7. thin	8. thank you

再練習這些以 /θ/ 結尾的字：

1. teeth
2. mouth
3. faith
4. Smith
5. path
6. month

接下來請仔細做這個對照練習：

1. think — sink
2. sin — thin
3. thing — sing
4. sick — thick
5. theme — seem
6. sank — thank
7. face — faith
8. mouth — mouse
9. pass — path
10. myth — miss
11. moss — moth
12. youth — use〔jus〕

再跟著唸以下的句子，分別出差異所在：

1. Miss Smith is sinking. — Miss Smith is thinking.
2. His face is strong. — His faith is strong.
3. It's a good pass. — It's a good path.
4. It's a bit sick. — It's a bit thick.
5. What a nice mouse！— What a nice mouth！
6. The theme seems thin.
7. That thing is too thick.
8. The cat has a mouse in its mouth.
9. Miss Smith has nice teeth.

在同一句中有 /θ/、/s/ 連接的情形，也得特別練習：

1. The nor*th s*ide of town.
2. The sou*th s*ide of town.
3. Miss Smi*th s*its here.
4. Thi*s th*ing is mine.
5. The bo*ss th*inks so.

12 ⑩ /s/、/θ/ 的練習

（a）練習唸以下的數字：

$$6 = [\text{ sıks }]$$

$$66 = [\text{ sıkstı sıks }]$$

$$666 = [\text{ sıks hʌndrəd ən sıkstı sıks }]$$

$$6,666 = [\text{ sıks θauzənd sıks hʌndrəd ən sıkstı sıks }]$$

$$66,666 = [\text{ sıkstı sıks θauzənd sıks hʌndrəd ən sıkstı sıks}]$$

(b) **對話練習**

A : My sister got sick yesterday.

B : Which sister ?

A : The sixteen-year-old.

B : Anything serious ?

A : I don't think so. Something like a cold, maybe.

≪**Coffee Break** ≫

What is the difference between a cat and a comma ?

→ *A cat has claws at the end of its paws, while*

    the comma has its pause at the end of its clause.

一隻貓和一個逗點之間有什麼不同呢 ?

→ 貓的腳掌末端有爪子，而逗點在子句後停頓 。

✦你是不是已經發現了一個有趣的現象 ?

    claws [klɔz] 爪 和 *clause* (子句) 同音 ; 而 *paws* [pɔz]
腳 和 *pause* (停止、休止) 同音。能夠將這個有趣的發音現象組成
一個謎語和解答，的確很不容易。你是否也想試試看能不能找出類似
的組合 ?

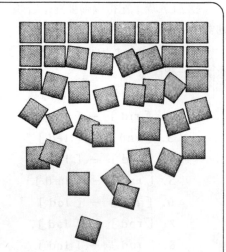

LESSON 13

本課主要在討論母音後的 /r/，以及
字中的 /r/，如 very的發音。接下來
還有一個區分中母音（/ʌ/, /ɑ/, /ɝ/
等），及其跟/r/結合後發音的練習。

13 ① 母音加上 / r / 以及 / l / 的練習

發 / r / 時，記得嘴形要圓，舌頭後捲，但不要碰到上顎。發 / l / 時，則要把舌前部份抵住上齒齦。

把母音插入〔 r — d 〕〔 l — d 〕當中，反覆唸下面的字，先一行行唸，再一欄欄唸。

1. 〔 rid 〕	— 〔 lid 〕	read	— lead
2. 〔 rɪd 〕	— 〔 lɪd 〕	rid	— lid
3. 〔 red 〕	— 〔 led 〕	raid	— laid
4. 〔 rɛd 〕	— 〔 lɛd 〕	red	— led
5. 〔 ræd 〕	— 〔 læd 〕	....	— lad
6. 〔 rɑd 〕	— 〔 lɑd 〕	rod	— ....
7. 〔 rɔd 〕	— 〔 lɔd 〕	rawed	— lawed
8. 〔 rod 〕	— 〔 lod 〕	road	— load
9. 〔 rʊd 〕	— 〔 lʊd 〕	....	— ....
10. 〔 rud 〕	— 〔 lud 〕	rude	— lewd

13 ② 母音後 / r / 的發音

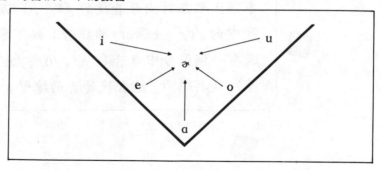

母音後 / r / 的音，和 / ɚ / 相近，如果能正確地發 / ɚ /，以下的 / ɪr /、/ ɛr /、/ ɑr /、/ or /、/ ur / 就不成問題了。

練習以下的生字：

    1. / i → ɚ → iɚ → ɪr / ⇨ peer

    2. / e → ɚ → eɚ → ɛr / ⇨ pair

3. / ɑ → ɚ → ɑɚ → ɑr / ⇨ par

4. / o → ɚ → oɚ → or / ⇨ pore

5. / u → ɚ → uɚ → ʊr / ⇨ poor

再練習下列的單字：

/ ɝ /		/ ɪr /		/ ɛr /		/ ɑr /		/ or /		/ ʊr /
purr	—	peer	—	pair	—	par	—	pour	—	poor
bird	—	beard	—	bared	—	barred	—	bored		
fur	—	fear	—	fair	—	far	—	four		

13 ③ 母音後 / r / 發音的練習

要儘量避免把 / r / 唸成長長的 / ɑ / 。

（a）練習 ear 中的 / ɪr /

先把 / ɪ + r / 分開唸，再合成一個音節，不要發成 / ɪ + ɑ / 。

1. we're 〔wɪr〕　　　　2. here 〔hɪr〕

3. beer 〔bɪr〕　　　　4. fear 〔fɪr〕

5. near 〔nɪr〕　　　　6. engineer 〔ˌɛndʒəˈnɪr〕

7. We're here.　　　　8. We're near.

9. We're engineers.　　10. The beer's here.

（b）練習 air 中的 / ɛr /

先把 / ɛ + r / 分開唸，再合成一個音節唸，不要發成 / ɛ + ɑ / 。

1. hair　　　　　　　2. care

3. fair　　　　　　　4. where 〔hwɛr〕

5. there　　　　　　　6. share

7. It's not fair.　　　8. I don't care.

再練習以下的問答：

chair

Where's my chair ?　〔hwɛrz maɪ ˈtʃɛr〕

There it is.　　　　〔ˈðɛr ɪt ɪz〕

代換：

1. book　　　　2. pen　　　　　3. bag
4. eraser　　　5. pencil　　　　6. hat

(c) 練習 are 中的 / ɑr /

先把 / ɑ + r / 分開唸，再合成一個音節唸。

1. are　　　2. car　　　3. far　　　4. hard
5. heart　　6. smart　　7. artist　　8. farmer
9. carpenter　　　10. How are you ?
11. Park the car in the yard.
12. Mark's a hardworking farmer.

(d) 練習 or 中的 / ɔr / 以及 ore 中的 / or /

1. door　　2. four　　3. more　　4. store
5. warm　　6. worn　　7. born　　8. morning
9. quarter　　10. Good morning, George.
11. Pour four more beers.
12. The store is warm in the morning.

(e) 練習 your 中的 / ʊr /

1. your　　2. sure　　3. poor　　4. cure
5. tour　　6. pure　　7. You're sure.
8. You're a poor tourist.

13 ④ / r / 前母音的代換

　　　　You're a good student. 〔 jʊrə.... 〕
we　　We're good students.　〔 wir .... 〕 或〔 wɪr .... 〕
they　They're good students.　〔 ðer.... 〕 或〔 ðɛr.... 〕

代換：

1. workers　2. you're a　3. hard　　4. they
5. poor　　6. tourists　7. we　　　8. teacher
9. you're a　10. hardworking　11. engineer 12. they

13 ⑤　字中 / r / 的發音

　　我們以 very 爲例，唸這個字時，先唸 /vɛr/，再加上 /rɪ/。這麼一來就包含兩個 /r/：一個在母音之後，一個在母音之前。練習唸唸看，速度由慢漸快：

　　　　/ vɛr — rɪ / , / vɛr — rɪ / , / vɛrrɪ / = very

以同樣的方式唸：

　　1. Mary / mɛr — rɪ /　　　　2. carry / kær — rɪ /
　　3. berry / bɛr — rɪ /　　　　4. cherry / tʃɛr — rɪ /
　　5. necessary /ˈnɛs — əs — sɛr — rɪ /

　　接下來把 sorry 分開來唸 / sɑr — rɪ /，並反覆練習幾次，最後，練習以下的句子：

　　1. Mary's sorry.　　　　2. Mary's very sorry.
　　3. It's very necessary.

13 ⑥　/ʌ/ 、/ɑ/ 、/ɝ/ 以及 /ɑr/ 的比較

　　練習唸下列的單字，直到能清楚辨別他們的差異爲止：

/ʌ/	/ɑ/	/ɝ/	/ɑr/
hut	hot	hurt	heart

再反覆唸以下的單字，先一欄欄唸，再一行行唸：

1.	2.	3.	4.
/ʌ/	/ɑ/	/ɝ/	/ɑr/
hut	hot	hurt	heart
shut	shot	shirt	—
luck	lock	lurk	lark
shucks	shocks	shirks	sharks
bun	—	burn	barn

接著練習這些句子：

　　1. He shut it.　　　— 　He shot it.　　　　　　/ʌ—ɑ/
　　2. He gave me a shot. — 　He gave me a shirt.　/ɑ—ɝ/
　　3. I want a pot.　　 — 　I want a part.　　　　/ɑ—ɑr/
　　4. This is my buddy. — 　This is my birdie.　　/ʌ—ɝ/
　　5. I like this firm.　 — 　I like this farm.　　　/ɝ—ɑr/

~~~《 Coffee Break 》~~~~~~~~~~~~~~

What color would you paint the sun and the wind?

→ *The sun rose and the wind blue.*

你會把太陽和風畫成什麼顏色?

→ 太陽用玫瑰紅,風用藍色。

~~~~~~~~~~~~~~~~~~~~

✦為什麼太陽要塗玫瑰紅,而風要塗藍的呢?多唸幾次 The sun *rose* and the wind *blue.* 是不是可以寫成 The sun *rose* and the wind *blew.*(太陽昇起而風吹著)。這又是一則想像力配合發音所產生的妙趣!

rose〔roz〕*vi.* 升起(rise 的過去式)　*n.* 玫瑰
blew〔blu〕*vi.* 吹(blow 的過去式)

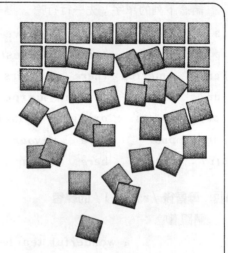

LESSON 14

本課再複習 /r/ 在母音後的發音，也
介紹滑音 /w/，並利用 /w/ 的嘴型，
進一步討論 /r/ 的發音。最後加上
/r/ — /l/ 的對照練習。

14 1 母音後 / r / 的發音

請唸下列的單字，先一行行唸，再一欄欄唸：

/ ɝ / :	w**or**k	h**ir**d	n**er**ve	j**our**ney	ch**ur**ch
/ ɚ / :	act**or**	teach**er**	ancest**or**	col**or**	fav**or**
/ ɛr / :	Am**er**ica	th**ere**	ch**air**s	f**air**	h**air**
/ ɑr / :	ch**ar**ts	f**ar**mer	c**ar**penter	ap**ar**tment	dep**ar**tment
/ ɔr / :	sp**or**ts	**or**anges	f**or**mal	qu**ar**ter	d**or**mitory
/ ʊr / :	p**oor**	s**ure**	y**our**	c**ure**	t**our**ist
/ ɪr / :	b**eer**	h**ere**	n**ear**	y**ear**	engin**eer**

14 2 母音後 / r / 、/ l / 的練習

請跟著唸：

a wonderful teacher

He's a wonderful teacher.

They're 'all wonderful teachers.

a beautiful girl

She's a beautiful girl.

They're 'all beautiful girls.

a terrible speaker

He's a terrible speaker.

They're 'all terrible speakers.

代換：

1. a careful doctor
2. a dull teacher
3. a wonderful girl
4. a tall pitcher
5. a skillful worker
6. a small nurse
7. a careful farmer
8. a bald barber

14 ③ /w/ 的發音

發 wood 中的 /wʊ/ 時，嘴型的變化

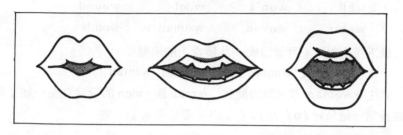

發 /w/ 之前，先將嘴　　發 /w/ 時將嘴唇　　發 /ʊ/ 的嘴型，比
唇縮起來。　　　　　　放鬆。　　　　　　　/w/ 稍圓一些。

　　/w/ 是一個滑音，發音時嘴唇突出成圓形，中間留一點空隙，讓氣息通過，振動聲帶。

　　/w/ 這個音是靠嘴唇發的，在唸下列每一個字時，都得注意嘴型：

　　　　/ wi，we，wɑ，wo，wu /
　　　　we　way　wa　woe　woo

模仿錄音帶的發音再唸幾次：

　　　　/ wi，we，wɑ，wo，wu /

練習 / w / 跟前母音或中母音合在一起的發音：

　　　　/ wi，we，wɑ /

　　請注意 / w / 跟後母音在一起發時（如 / ɔ /、/ o /、/ ʊ /、/ u /），嘴唇得做兩次變動：一次發 / w /，一次發後母音。

　　讓我們先練習 woe〔wo〕及 woo〔wu〕，開始時慢慢唸，再進入正常的速度：

　　　　/ w—o /，/ w—o /，/ wo /，/ wo /
　　　　/ w—u /，/ w—u /，/ wu /，/ wu /

　　當你能正確地發 / wo / 及 / wu / 時，再練習以下的單字：

/ɔ/	/o/	/ʊ/	/u/
walk	woke	wood	wooed
wall	won't	wool	wound
water	woven	woman	womb

以下這兩對單字可能造成一些發音上的困難：

　1. woman〔'wʊmən〕— women〔'wɪmən〕

　請注意woman 單複數的變化，-man 跟 -men 的發音完全一樣，差別在於第一個母音 /ʊ/ 及 /ɪ/。再反覆唸幾次。

　2. want〔wɑnt〕— won't〔wont〕

won't 是will not 的縮寫，再練習幾次這一對生字。

　接著練習以下的句子：

1. I won't walk home.　　2. He won't walk home.

3. We won't walk home.　4. The woman's walking.

5. The women're working. 6. The woman's working.

7. The women're walking. 8. The wood's wet.

9. The wool's wet.　　　10. The wool's on the wall.

11. The woman woke up.　12. The woman wants the wood.

13. That woman won't wear wool.

14 ④ 字首 / r / 的發音

　　　發 / r / 時舌頭的位置　　　發 / w / 的嘴型

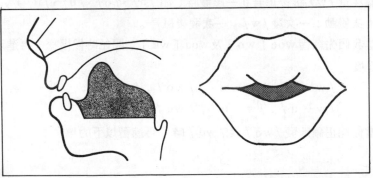

　　在唸一些字首是 /r/ 的字時，因爲發 /r/ 的嘴型是圓的，與 /w/ 的嘴型類似，所以，利用 /w/ 的嘴型，再把舌頭往後捲來發 /r/ 的音，有助於掌握字首 /r/ 的正確發音。

1. weed — read　　　　　2. wait — rate

3. wed — red　　　　　　4. wake — rake

5. wax — racks　　　　　6. woe — row

7. womb　　　　　　　　8. wooed — rude

　　現在，先唸有 /r/ 的音節，再把整個片語唸出來：

1. /rɛ — ro/　a red rose　　2. /rɛ — ru/　a red room

3. /raɪ — ru/　the right room　4. /raɪ — ro/ the right road

5. /rɔ — ro/　the wrong road 6. /ri — raɪ/ read and write

　　再練習以下的句子：

1. I'm reading a red book.　2. I'm writing in my room.

3. I'm eating red rice.　　　4. I took the wrong road.

14 ⑤　字首 /l/ 的發音

發 /l/ 時的位置圖

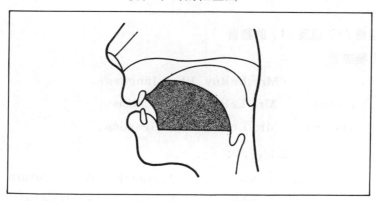

　　參照上圖，用舌前抵住上齒齦，重複下列練習。

/ li, le, lɑ, lo, lu, laɪ /

再練習以下的片語跟句子：

1. / lɔ — laɪ / a long line　　2. / lo — le / a low lake

3. / lɔ — li / 　a long leap　　4. / lɑ — lo / a large loaf

5. I like love letters.　　6. She's a lovely little lady.

7. It's a long, long way to London.

14 ⑥ 字首 / r / 、/ l / 的比較

練習以下的單字，從左唸到右，再從右唸到左：

1. read — lead	2. rate — late
3. rake — lake	4. red — led
5. rock — lock	6. rust — lust
7. raw — law	8. wrong — long
9. road — load	10. rook — look
11. room — loom	12. right — light
13. ride — lied	14. rice — lice
15. arrive — alive	16. river — liver
17. correct — collect	18. Paris — palace

14 ⑦ 字首 / r / 以及 / l / 的發音

（a）代換練習

　　　　　　　　Mr. LeRoy likes language.

radios　　Mr. LeRoy likes radios.

lessons　　Mr. LeRoy likes lessons.

利用以下的單字繼續練習：

1. rain	2. roses	3. lunch	4. literature
5. records	6. London	7. rice	8. lemons
9. rivers	10. life	11. rest	12. ladies
13. letters	14. restaurants	15. rules	16. lakes

(b) **聽力練習**

仔細聽下列各組句子，並重複一次：

1. Go to the right.
   Go to the light.

2. I hate rice.
   I hate lice.

3. He's a good reader.
   He's a good leader.

4. It's a big rake.
   It's a big lake.

5. This is the wrong pencil.
   This is the long pencil.

6. They rent a car.
   They lent a car.

7. The river is bad.
   The liver is bad.

8. He corrected the homework.
   He collected the homework.

≪Coffee Break≫

Which is the strongest day of the week ?

→ *It's Sunday, because all the rest are weak days.*

一星期中最強壯的是哪一天？

→ 是星期天，因為其他的都是弱的日子。

✦ 這是一則有趣而簡易的謎語。相信你一看便知道最有趣的地方在哪裏：在 *weak* 〔wik〕弱的 與 *week* 星期 同音。這不是很好玩嗎？相信你有許多更有趣的點子，你不妨把它寫下來。

≪ Coffee Break ≫

What musical instrument should we never believe ?
→ *A lyre*.

那一種樂器我們決不應相信？
→ 古希臘的豎琴。

✦你是否想過世界上有永遠不能令人相信的樂器呢？你是否覺得奇怪，世界上竟然會有說謊的樂器？請你從發音上去想，哪個字和 *lyre* 〔 laɪr 〕*n.* 古希臘豎琴 音相似？是 *liar* 〔'laɪɚ〕說謊的人。

這不是很有意思嗎？由於文字的聯想，使我們發現，世界上有「說謊的樂器」！

≪ Coffee Break ≫

What vegetable needs a plumber ?
→ *Leek*.

什麼青菜需要水管工人？
→ 韭

✦照理說，需要水管工人的應該是在漏水（leak）的時候。

怎麼會有需要水管工人的青菜（vegetable）呢？原來，leak 與 leek（韭）讀起來沒有差別。

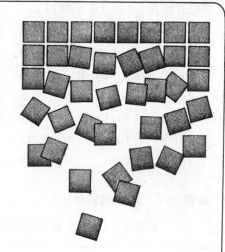

LESSON 15

本課先複習 /s/－/ʃ/ 的對照，以及 /z+ʃ/ 的發音。接下來討論不定冠詞與以母音起首的字結合後的唸法。最後，再針對單複數變換做更多的練習。

15 ① 利用母音表練習

把母音插入〔f — l〕中練習。

1. 〔fil〕 = feel   2. 〔fɪl〕 = fill
3. 〔fel〕 = fail   4. 〔fɛl〕 = fell
5. 〔fæl〕在 fallacy 中   6. 〔fʌl〕(沒有意義)
7. 〔fɝl〕 = furl   8. 〔fɔl〕 = fall
9. 〔fol〕 = foal   10. 〔fʊl〕 = full
11. 〔ful〕 = fool   12. 〔faɪl〕= fiie
13. 〔faʊl〕= foul   14. 〔fɔɪl〕= foil

15 ② 複習 / s / 、 / ʃ / 的對照

虛線是 / ʃ / 的位置，實線是 / s / 的位置

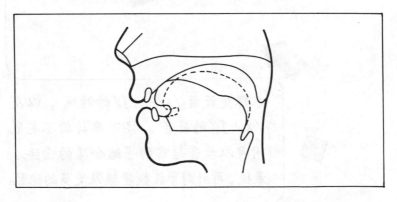

請唸以下各對單字及句子，先從右唸到左，再從左唸到右：

1. sue — shoe   2. suit — shoot   3. so — show
4. same — shame   5. sell — shell   6. sip — ship
7. sift — shift   8. see — she   9. seep — sheep
10. seed — she'd   11. seal — she'll   12. seen — sheen
13. She should sew it.   —   She should show it.
14. She should sell it. —   She should shell it.
15. She should sift it. —   She should shift it.
16. She should sip it.   —   She should ship it.

15 ③ Does she，Is she，Was she 的練習

記住 / ʃ / 前面的 / z / 變成 / ʒ / ， / s / 變成 / ʃ / ，也就是：

Does she … ?	發成 / dʌʒʃi /
Is she … ?	發成 / ɪʒʃi /
Was she … ?	發成 / wəʒʃi /
Yes, she … ?	發成 / jɛʃʃi /

先練習以下的問答：

see the sea
Does she see the sea ?
Yes, she sees the sea.

study English
Does she study English ?
Yes, she studies English.

代換：

1. play tennis
2. like ice cream
3. live in Japan
4. understand us
5. need a pen
6. want a rest
7. have a watch
8. know the answer
9. like music

再練習　Is she，Was she：

busy now
Is she busy now ?
Yes, she is.

yesterday
Was she busy yesterday ?
Yes, she was.

代換：

1. sick
2. tired
3. now
4. O.K.
5. yesterday
6. at home
7. now
8. happy
9. yesterday

15 4 母音前的不定冠詞

先唸以下兩個片語：

a name 〔 ə-nem 〕

an aim 〔 ə-nem 〕

兩者發音基本上相同，我們可以把不定冠詞 an 字尾的 / n / ，跟其後的母音相連結。請做以下的練習：

album — " nalbum " — a " nalbum " — It's a " nalbum."

ashtray — " nashtray " — a " nashtray " — It's a " nashtray. "

envelope — " nenvelope " — a " nenvelope " — It's a "nenvelope."

egg — " negg " — a " negg " — It's a " negg."

overcoat — "novercoat" — a "novercoat" — It's a " novercoat. "

exercise — " nexercise " — a " nexercise " — It's a " nexercise."

American — "namerican" — a "namerican" — He's a " namerican."

engineer — "nengineer" — a "nengineer" — He's a " nengineer."

old man — "nold" man — a " nold " man — He's a "nold" man.

同樣地也把 / n / 加在以下各片語之前：

1. important person
2. interesting teacher
3. angry man
4. awful student
5. office worker
6. efficient worker
7. important teacher
8. interesting student
9. old friend
10. important engineer
11. awful doctor
12. interesting young man

代換練習：

Bob's an American.

engineer　Bob's an engineer.

old man　Bob's an old man.

最後，還有一項重要的練習，你必須想清楚，什麼時候用 / ə / 或用 / ne / ，甚至在碰到不接名詞的形容詞及複數名詞時 ， / ə / 、 / ne / 都不可以用：

```
                    Mary's a student.
    American        Mary's an American.
    they            They're Americans.
    angry           They're angry.
    Bob             Bob's angry.
```

代換：

1. important	2. Englishman	3. carpenter
4. we	5. you're a	6. engineer
7. office worker	8. they	9. old
10. old men	11. he	12. teacher
13. awful	14. awful teacher	15. they
16. important	17. important persons	18. she
19. artist	20. old	21. old lady
22. they	23. engineers	24. my father

15 5 單複數變換

（a）從單數變成複數或從複數變成單數：

```
        That guy's a student.
        Those guys're students.
        These kids want cokes.
        This kid wants a coke.
```

繼續以下的單複數變換：

1. That's a cheap place.
2. Those students live here.
3. This is a hard lesson.
4. These're hard lessons.
5. Those kids need books.
6. This ticket's expensive.
7. That man has a gun.
8. That guy's a crook.
9. These girls study hard.
10. Those're my pencils.
11. That student doesn't study.
12. These lessons aren't easy.
13. Those guys don't know English.

14. That girl's a guide.

15. This student repeats everything.

16. This exercise is very hard.

(b) 代換練習

	This is a book.
ticket	This is a ticket.
those	Those're tickets.
guides	Those're guides.
bag	That's a bag.
this	This is a bag.
sweaters	These're sweaters.

繼續：

1. eggs	2. that	3. newspapers
4. these	5. picture	6. my friend
7. those	8. records	9. that
10. album	11. these	12. suits
13. this	14. birds	15. that
16. overcoats	17. this	18. sheet
19. those	20. machine	21. these

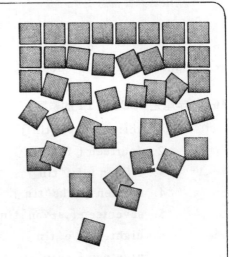

LESSON 16

本課將做許多有關數字與日期的練習,
並特別強調 /tɪ/ 跟 /tin/ 的區別, 也
討論序數後 th 的發音。其次還有 /z/
與 /ð/ 的對照 , 以及在 /ð/ 之前 /s/,
/z/ 的發音。

16 1 複習字尾的 / n /

請跟著錄音帶唸 :

1. teen	2. tin	3. pain	4. pen
5. tan	6. ton	7. turn	8. gone
9. phone	10. spoon	11. fine	12. town

16 2 字尾是 TEEN 或 TY 的數字

1. thirteen〔θɝˊtin〕 — thirty〔ˊθɝtɪ〕
2. fourteen〔forˊtin〕 — forty〔ˊfortɪ〕
3. fifteen〔fɪfˊtin〕 — fifty〔ˊfɪftɪ〕
4. sixteen〔sɪksˊtin〕 — sixty〔ˊsɪkstɪ〕
5. seventeen〔ˌsɛvənˊtin〕— seventy〔ˊsɛvəntɪ〕
6. eighteen〔eˊtin〕 — eighty〔ˊetɪ〕
7. nineteen〔naɪnˊtin〕 — ninety〔ˊnaɪntɪ〕

練習以下的例句 :

Which is more, thirteen or thirty ?
Thirty is more than thirteen.

請繼續練習其他的數字 。

16 3 序數的發音

所有的序數字尾都有 / θ / 這個音 , 只有第一、第二、第三除外 :

1. first〔fɝst〕	2. second〔ˊsɛkənd〕
3. third〔θɝd〕	4. fourth〔forθ〕
5. fifth〔fɪfθ〕	6. sixth〔sɪksθ〕
7. seventh〔ˊsɛvənθ〕	8. eighth〔etθ〕 （特別注意）
9. ninth〔naɪnθ〕	10. tenth〔tɛnθ〕
11. eleventh〔ɪˊlɛvənθ〕	12. twelfth〔twɛlfθ〕
13. thirteenth〔ˊθɝˊtinθ〕	14. fourteenth〔ˊforˊtinθ〕
15. fifteenth〔ˊfɪfˊtinθ〕	16. sixteenth〔ˊsɪksˊtinθ〕

17. seventeenth〔ˈsɛvənˈtinθ〕　18. eighteenth〔ˈeˈtinθ〕

19. nineteenth〔ˈnaɪnˈtinθ〕　20. twentieth〔ˈtwɛntɪɪθ〕

21. twenty-first〔ˈtwɛntɪˌfɝst〕

22. twenty-second〔ˈtwɛntɪsɛkənd〕　23. thirtieth〔ˈθɝtɪɪθ〕

24. thirty-first〔ˈθɝtɪfɝst〕

16 ④ 年代、月份及日期

(a) When were you born？你什麼時候出生？

　　　　When were you born？

　　　　I was born in 1970.

可以自己選擇幾個年份練習。

(b) When's your birthday？你哪一天生日？

　　　　在回答之前，先練習日期的說法：

1. the first of January　　〔ðə fɝst əv ˈdʒænjʊˌɛrɪ〕

2. the second of February　〔ðə ˈsɛkənd əv ˈfɛbrʊˌɛrɪ〕

3. the third of March　　　〔ðə ˈθɝd əv martʃ〕

4. the fourth of April　　　〔ðə forθ əv ˈeprəl〕

5. the twelfth of May　　　〔ðə twɛlfθ əv me〕

6. the fifteenth of June　　〔ðə fɪfˈtinθ əv dʒun〕

7. the twentieth of July　　〔ðə ˈtwɛntɪɪθ əv dʒuˈlaɪ〕

8. the twenty-fifth of August〔ðə ˈtwɛntɪfɪfθ əv ˈɔgəst〕

9. the thirtieth of September〔ðəˈθɝtɪɪθ əv sɛpˈtɛmbɚ〕

10. the thirty-first of October〔ðəˈθɝtɪ fɝst əv akˈtobɚ〕

　　　記住 / əv / 發得很快很輕，而且還跟前面的子音結合，如：

　　　　　first of　 ＝〔fɝs-təv〕

　　　　　second of ＝〔ˈsɛkən-dəv〕

　　　　　twelfth of ＝〔ˈtwɛlf-θəv〕

　　　接下來再做問答練習，可以隨便選擇幾個日期回答：

　　　　　When's your birthday？

　　　　　It's the … of …

16 5   / z / 與 / ð / 的對照

/ z / 的位置圖   / ð / 的位置圖

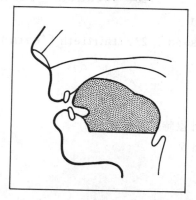 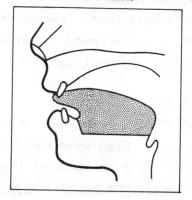

我們已經做過 /θ/ 及 / s / 的對照，現在再做 /ð/ 及 / z / 的對照：

Zen〔zɛn〕— then〔ðɛn〕

breeze〔briz〕— breathe〔brið〕

練習以下這二個句子。

He studied Zen. — He studied then.

16 6   / s + ð / 以及 / z + ð / 的發音

發 / s /、/ z /（實線）+ / ð /（虛線）時舌頭的移動

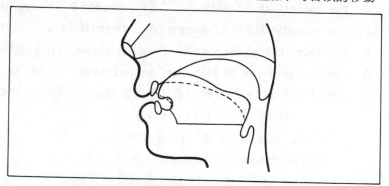

有些常見的片語用到 /s＋ð/，/z＋ð/，如：

Is the ... ?	〔 ɪz ðə 〕
Was the ... ?	〔 wəz ðə 〕
Does the ... ?	〔 dʌz ðə 〕
... has the ... ?	〔 hæz ðə 〕
... wants the ...	〔 wɑnts ðə 〕
... likes the ...	〔 laɪks ðə 〕

在唸這些字時，舌頭必須迅速地從發 /s/、/z/ 的位置，移到發 /ð/ 的位置。先慢慢練習舌頭的移動，加快後自然可以唸得正確。/s/、/z/ 之後 /ð/ 的發音，不如單獨發 /ð/ 時講究，如上圖所示，舌頭只需輕觸上齒內部即可。

首先，讓我們先練習延長後 /z/、/ð/ 的發音：

〔 ɪz —— ð — ə 〕

再逐漸加快速度回復正常的發音：

〔 ɪz — ð — ə 〕，〔 ɪz- ð-ə 〕，〔 ɪzðə 〕

以同樣的方式練習其他的片語。

16 ⑦ /ð/ 之後 /s/、/z/ 發音的練習

（a）/s/＋/ð/ 的代換練習

	He wants the house.
visits	He visits the house.
office	He visits the office.

代換：

1. likes　　2. beer　　3. desk　　4. wants

5. keys　　6. keeps　　7. room　　8. visits

（b）/z/＋/ð/ 的問答練習

dictionary ... useful

Is that dictionary useful ?

Yes, very useful.

代換：

1. book ... interesting   2. girl ... busy

3. chair ... hard   4. man ... important

5. class ... necessary   6. word ... difficult

7. textbook ... easy   8. coat ... warm

(c) does the 以及 is the 的問答練習

     rich

    Is the teacher rich ?

    Yes, he / she is.（No, he / she isn't.）

    like the students

    Does the teacher like the students ?

    Yes, he / she does.（No, he / she doesn't.）

代換：

1. careful   2. laugh   3. lucky

4. steal   5. lazy   6. run

7. late   8. rude   9. remember names

10. crazy   11. listen to records   12. read Japanese

(d) use the 的代換練習

                 I often use the subway.

   he   He often uses the subway.

  the typewriter   He often uses the typewriter.

代換：

1. we   We often use the typewriter.

2. the language lab   We often use the language lab.

3. Allen   Allen often use the language lab.

4. these books   Allen often uses these books.

5. they   They often use these books.

6. that piano   They often use that piano.

7. she   She often uses that piano.
8. this camera   She often uses this camera.
9. those pens   She often uses those pens.

(e) 包含 /z/ + /ð/ 直敍句改爲問句的練習

This is the new lesson.
Is this the new lesson ?
The doctor uses that car.
Does the doctor use that car ?

繼續把以下的直敍句改爲問句:

1. That man lives here.   Does that man live here ?

2. That room's small.   Is that room small ?

3. The class was late.   Was the class late ?

4. That soup was good.   Was that soup good ?

5. The president uses   Does the president use the
   this office.   office ?

6. The secretary uses   Does the secretary use that
   that typewriter.   typewriter ?

7. She uses that copying   Does she use that copying
   machine too.   machine too ?

8. She always uses this   Does she always use this
   desk.   desk ?

~~~~~~~~ **Tongue Trippers 繞口令** ~~~~~~~~

I NEED not your needles,

They're needless to me,

For kneading of needles

were needless, you see ;

But did my neat trousers

But need to be kneed,

I then should have need

Of your needles indeed.

我不需要你的針，

它們對我沒用，

因為磨製針

是不需要的，你瞧；

但是我潔淨的褲子

却需因彎膝而碰觸，

我於是便的確需要

你的針。

needle [ˈnidḷ] *n.* 針　needless [ˈnidlɪs] *adj.* 無用的
knead [nid] *v.* 塑造；揑製　neat [nit] *adj.* 潔淨的
indeed [ɪnˈdid] *adv.* 確實

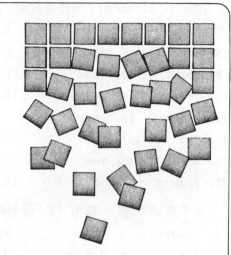

LESSON 17

本課主要在字首 /r/ ─ /l/ 發音的對
照，也包括 /r/, /l/ 在字首子音群
（如 play, pray 等字首爲連續二個以
上的子音）裏的對照比較。最後再提
供更進一步單複數問題的練習。

17 ① 複習字首 / r / 、 / l / 的比較

請唸以下這些有 / r / 的字或片語，記得嘴形要圓，舌頭要往後捲：

1. reads　　2. rid　　　3. raids　　　4. red

5. rats　　6. rots　　　7. wrong　　　8. wrote

9. rooks　10. rude　　11. rides　　12. rugs

13. repeats　14. recites　15. reviews　16. repairs

17. returns　18. remembers

19. Are you ready?　　20. the wrong road

21. a red riding hood　　22. a red rug

23. remember Rome　　24. repair the radio

接下來再練習一些有 / l / 的字或片語，記得把舌尖抵住上齒齦：

1. leader　　2. liver　　3. later　　4. letter

5. ladder　　6. locker　　7. lawn　　8. load

9. lower　10. look　　11. Luke　　12. lover

13. lighter　14. louder　15. loiter

16. a little lighter　　17. a little later

18. a little louder　　19. a little lower

20. Look at Luke.　　21. I like long letters.

22. Let's leave a little later.　23. Louise loves lilies.

利用下列各組單字，練習 / r / 及 / l / 的對照：

1. reader — leader　　2. river — liver

3. razor — laser　　4. ramp — lamp

5. rocker — locker　　6. wrong — long

7. road — load　　8. room — loom

9. writer — lighter　　10. arrive — alive

然後再跟著唸下面的句子：

1. Larry likes rice.　　2. Roger likes rice.

3. Louise loves Rome.　　4. Is this the right lighter?

5. The writer lost his lighter.　6. The leader's reading.

7. He corrected the collected papers.

8. He wrote a love letter in his room.

17 ② 有 /r/ 或 /l/ 的子音群

（a）子音＋/r/ 的發音

　　這種發音的組合可以在子音跟 /r/ 之間加上 /ə/，先獨立練習子音加 /ər/ 這一部份，熟悉之後再去掉 /ə/，你會發現子音＋/r/ 的發音其實並不難。請跟著錄音帶做這個練習：

/bər/ — /rɛd/ — /bərɛd/ — 〔brɛd〕	bread
/gər/ — /ro/ — /gəro/ — 〔gro〕	grow
/dər/ — /rɔ/ — /dərɔ/ — 〔drɔ〕	draw
/kər/ — /raɪm/ — /kəraɪm/ — 〔kraɪm〕	crime
/pər/ — /re/ — /pəre/ — 〔pre〕	pray
/tər/ — /rɪp/ — /tərɪp/ — 〔trɪp〕	trip
/fər/ — /rut/ — /fərut/ — 〔frut〕	fruit
/θər/ — /rɛd/ — /θərɛd/ — 〔θrɛd〕	thread
/skər/ — /ru/ — /skəru/ — 〔skru〕	screw
/ʃər/ — /ru/ — /ʃəru/ — 〔ʃru〕	shrew

（b）子音＋/l/

　　在這種情況下，就不能把 /ə/ 加進去。在發第一個子音時，必須已經把舌頭放在 /l/ 的位置。例如唸 play〔ple〕這個字，就保持舌頭在 /l/ 的位置，利用雙唇發 /p/ 的音。這麼一來，字首子音便幾乎跟 /l/ 同時發出，而沒有任何母音夾在中間。

　　請仔細地唸以下這些字：

blow — blue — glass — cloud — play — fly — flute

17③ 比較子音群中的 /r/、/l/

請跟著錄音帶反覆練習以下各組對比的生字：

1. brew — blue
2. bright — blight
3. crime — climb
4. crowd — cloud
5. grow — glow
6. grass — glass
7. prày — play
8. proud — plowed
9. free — flee
10. fry — fly
11. fruit — flute
12. fright — flight

17④ 單複數練習

（a） be 動詞的縮寫

單　數	複　數
1. The word's easy.	The words're easy.
2. The suit's nice.	The suits're nice.
3. The ticket's cheap.	The tickets're cheap.
4. The road's long.	The roads're long.
5. The store's open.	The stores're open.
6. The room's no good.	The rooms're no good.
7. The church is big.	The churches're big.
8. The rose's red.	The roses're red.
9. The pencil's short.	The pencils're short.
10. The kid's fine.	The kids're fine.
11. The bed's wet.	The beds're wet.
12. The concert's over.	The concerts're over.
13. The guide's late.	The guides're late.
14. The guy's crazy.	The guys're crazy.
15. The diamond's small.	The diamonds're small.
16. The lab's full.	The labs're full.
17. The record's loud.	The records're loud.
18. The side's wide.	The sides're wide.
19. The desk's hard.	The desks're hard.
20. The cost's high.	The costs're high.

(b) **s 移轉的練習**

單數（動詞＋s）	複數（主詞＋〔e〕s）
1. The bus stops here.	The buses stop here.
2. The student writes there.	The students write there.
3. The doctor lives there.	The doctors live there.
4. My friend works there.	My friends work there.
5. My friend walks there.	My friends walk there.
6. The girl plays there.	The girls play there.
7. The guide sits there.	The guides sit there.
8. The artist paints there.	The artists paint there.
9. The student practices there.	The students practice there.
10. The class studies there.	The classes study there.
11. The boy washes there.	The boys wash there.
12. The secretary types there.	The secretaries type there.
13. The teacher reads there.	The teachers read there.
14. The tourist eats there.	The tourists eat there.
15. The train leaves there.	The trains leave there.

(c) **敘述句改成問句**

The guide's late.

Is the guide late ?

The guides're late.

Are the guides late ?

The bus stops here.

Does the bus stop here ?

The buses stop here.

Do the buses stop here ?

代換：

1. The concert's over.

2. The doctors live there.

3. The records're loud.

4. The secretary types there.

5. The tourists eat there.

6. The guy's crazy.

7. The desks're hard.

8. The students practice English.

9. The teacher reads Japanese.

10. The roads're wide.

LESSON 18

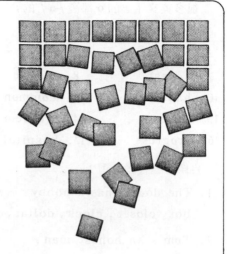

本課練習 /ɑ/ 以及 /ə/ 兩個母音,並做 /ɜ/ 和 /ɑr/ 的比較。接著,附加問句的練習有助於學習程度的瞭解。最後再複習子音群中 /r/,/l/ 的發音,以及單複數的變換。

18 ⒈ 利用母音表練習

很多英文字裏的 o 都發 /ɑ/ 的音，以下列出一些例子, 請跟著唸一次：

1. Bob	2. Tom	3. box
4. clock	5. not	6. on
7. honest	8. doctor	9. dollar
10. hobby	11. common	12. closet
13. concert	14. problem	15. popular
16. progress	17. hospital	18. economics

再做一些代換練習：

1. The doctor has a hobby.

   box, closet, clock, dollar, problem, hospital

2. Tom's an honest man.

   hot, common, popular, economical

3. Bob's not an honest man.

   hot, common, popular, economical

18 ⒉ 含 /ə/ 的字

/ə/ 是很常出現的一個母音，經常可以在輕音節裏看到它。以下列出一些發音有 /ə/ 的字，請跟著練習：

1. about	2. across	3. adult
4. afraid	5. again	6. ago
7. alone	8. along	9. American
10. arrive	11. potato	12. tomato
13. company	14. custom	15. delicious
16. secretary	17. machine	18. engine
19. president	20. beautiful	21. university
22. gentleman	23. gentlemen	24. pronounce

18 ③ /ɜ/ 跟 /ɑr/ 的對照

請唸下列各組單字，先從左唸到右，再從右唸到左：

/ɜ/	/ɑr/	/ɜ/	/ɑr/	/ɜ/	/ɑr/
stir — star		hurt — heart		firm — farm	
fur — far		bird — bard		burn — barn	
cur — car		heard — hard		shirk — shark	
purr — par		lurk — lark		surge — sarge	

再練習以下的句子：

1. Is it far by car?
2. The firm has a farm.
3. We heard a hard word.
4. Did they burn the barn?
5. Bart has a hard heart.
6. Marilyn was a great star.

接著，練習一些附加問句：

we're
We're smart students, aren't we?
Yes. We certainly are.

you're a
You're a smart student, aren't you?
Yes. I certainly am.

they aren't
They aren't smart students, are they?
No. They certainly aren't.

請繼續以下的練習（*pl*. 代表複數）

1. we aren't   We aren't smart students, are we?
2. they're   They're smart students, aren't they?
3. Mary and Joe   Mary and Joe are smart students, aren't they?
4. you aren't a   You aren't a smart student, are you?
5. we   We aren't smart students, are we?

6. you're a   You're a smart student, aren't you?

7. we're   We're smart students, aren't we?

8. you aren't (*pl.*)   You aren't smart students, are you?

9. they   They aren't smart students, are they?

10. Bill and I   Bill and I aren't smart students, are we?

11. you're (*pl.*)   You're smart students, aren't you?

12. you and Bob   You and Bob're smart students, aren't you?

18 4 /ɑ/、/ʌ/、/ɝ/ 及 /ɑr/ 的對照

/ɑ/	/ʌ/	/ɝ/	/ɑr/
hot	hut	hurt	heart
lock	luck	lurk	lark
cod	cud	curd	card
shocks	shucks	shirks	sharks
—	bun	burn	barn

18 5 子音群中的 /r/ 及 /l/

這個練習是接 17 課 3 的，先唸以下各對單字，從左唸到右，再從右唸到左：

/r/		/l/	/r/		/l/
pray	—	play	brush	—	blush
crowd	—	cloud	free	—	flee
crime	—	climb	fry	—	fly
grass	—	glass	fright	—	flight

然後比較這六對句子的差異：

The grass is green. — The glass is green.

I don't like crowds. — I don't like clouds.

He wants to pray. — He wants to play.

It was a terrible crime.　—　It was a terrible climb.

I had a bad fright.　—　I had a bad flight.

I saw a chicken fry.　—　I saw a chicken fly.

18 6 單複數練習

單 數	複 數
1. The student's studying.	The students're studying.
2. The doctor's working.	The doctors're working.
3. His friend's leaving now.	His friends're leaving now.
4. The girl's practicing.	The girls're practicing.
5. The bird's singing.	The birds're singing.
6. The teacher's reading.	The teachers're reading.
7. The guide's speaking.	The guides're speaking.
8. The nurse's going home.	The nurses're going home.
9. I'm wearing a tie.	We're wearing ties.
10. He's using a pen.	They're using pens.
11. She's wearing a ring.	They're wearing rings.
12. My friend's driving a car.	My friends're driving cars.
13. The secretary's using a typewriter.	The secretaries're using typewriters.
14. That student's writing a letter.	Those students're writing letters.
15. That girl's buying a present.	Those girls're buying presents.
16. That boy's wearing a sweater.	Those boys're wearing sweaters.

≪ **Coffee Break** ≫

What is the richest country in the world ?

→ *Ireland, because its capital is always Dublin.*

世界上最富有的國家是哪一個？

→ 愛爾蘭，因爲它的首都總是都柏林。

✦您是否覺得奇怪，爲什麼首都是都柏林的愛爾蘭會是世界上最富有的國家呢？道理很簡單，Dublin唸起來就像是doubling，是「加倍」的意思，而capital 除了作「首都」之外，還有「資金；資本」的意思。資本加倍的多，當然是最富有了。

≪ **Coffee Break** ≫

Why a vote in Congress vote like a cold ?

→ *Because sometimes the ayes have it, and some-times the no's.*

爲什麼在國會中投票就像感冒一樣？

→ 因爲有時贊成的佔多數，有時反對的佔多數。

✦ ayes and no's 唸起來不是很像 *eyes and nose* 嗎？感冒的時候不是常一把鼻涕一把淚的（ eyes and nose ），那像不像是投票（ ayes and no's ）呢？

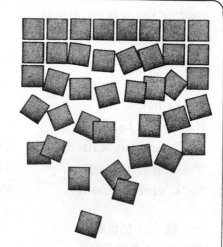

LESSON 19

本課先比較 /ɔ/ 及 /o/ 這兩個母音,
再利用附加問句,練習 /r/, /l/ 的
發音,以取代單純的發音練習。最
後的單複數變化,提供單複數兩種不
同的練習,以熟練發音及句型。

19 ① /l/ 之前 /ɔ/、/o/ 兩個母音的比較

請練習以下兩組相互對照的句子：

/ɔ/	/o/
1. He has a ball.	He has a bowl.
2. It's a small hall.	It's a small hole.
3. I like her stall.	I like her stole.
4. He's very bald.	He's very bold.
5. The man was called.	The man was cold.
6. The horse is falling.	The horse is foaling.
7. He's getting balder.	He's getting bolder.

19 ② /ʊ/ 跟 /u/ 的對照

請練習以下各對單字：

/ʊ/	/u/		/ʊ/	/u/
soot	suit		would	wooed
could	cooed		pull	pool
look	Luke		full	fool

再唸以下的句子：

1. Look at Luke.　　　　2. This is good food.
3. That's a good suit.　　4. She's a good cook.
5. He's in a good mood.　6. That's a rude look.
7. The pool is full.　　　8. This school is full of fools.

現在請利用上面列出來的生字，做一個對照問答練習，如：

> pool
> Did he/she say pull?
> No. He/she said pool.

> full
> Did he/she say fool?
> No. He/she said full.

19 ③ /r/、/l/ 在子音群裏的對照

Did you say grass ?

No. I said glass.

Did you say cloud ?

No. I said crowd.

以同樣的方式，繼續以下的比較：

1. grow	2. brew	3. cloud	4. fry
5. play	6. blue	7. class	8. grass
9. crowd	10. bright	11. flee	12. grass
13. proud	14. blessed	15. blight	16. pray
17. crass	18. flight	19. fruit	20. crime

19 ④ 包含 /r/ 或 /l/ 的附加問句

（a）肯定句的附加問句

play baseball

He plays baseball, doesn't he ?

have a tape recorder

He has a tape recorder, doesn't he ?

繼續以下的練習：

1. speak good English   He speaks good English, doesn't he ?

2. help the president   He helps the president, doesn't he ?

3. live in the country   He lives in the country, doesn't he ?

4. speak French   He speaks French, doesn't he ?

5. sleep on Friday   He sleeps on Friday, doesn't he ?

6. she   She sleeps on Friday, doesn't she ?

7. eat fruit   She eats fruit, doesn't she ?

8. like history   She likes history, doesn't she ?

9. take photographs   She takes photographs, doesn't she ?

10. they   They take photographs, don't they ?

11. practice every day	They practice every day, don't they?
12. listen to the English programs	They listen to the English programs, don't they?
13. sometimes take trips	They sometimes take trips, don't they?
14. you	You sometimes take trips, don't you?
15. always take the train	You always take the train, don't you?
16. sometimes take the plane	You sometimes take the plane, don't you?
17. write love letters	You sometimes write love letters, don't you?
18. often eat fruit	You often eat fruit, don't you?
19. often play the flute	You often play the flute, don't you?
20. sometimes forget English words	You sometimes forget English words, don't you?

(b) 否定句的附加問句

wear glove

He doesn't wear gloves, does he?

have a clean plate

He doesn't have a clean plate, does he?

繼續以下的練習：

1. plan his work	He doesn't plan his work, does he?
2. sleep at home	He doesn't sleep at home, does he?
3. get angry	He doesn't get angry, does he?
4. swim in April	He doesn't swim in April, does he?
5. she	She doesn't swim in April, does she?
6. like the teacher	She doesn't like the teacher, does she?

7. wear a brooch	She doesn't wear a brooch, does she ?
8. see her friends now	She doesn't see her friends now, does she ?
9. have a hair brush	She doesn't have a hair brush, does she ?
10. dress well	She doesn't dress well, does she ?
11. like France	She doesn't like France, does she ?
12. you	You don't like France, do you ?
13. come from Rome	You don't come from Rome, do you ?
14. eat fried rice	You don't eat fried rice, do you ?
15. have any fresh fruit	You don't have any fresh fruit, do you ?
16. never play football	You never play football, do you ?
17. they	They never play football, do they ?
18. travel	They never travel, do they ?
19. have trouble	They never have trouble, do they ?
20. clean the streets	They never clean the streets, do they ?

19 5　單複數練習

以下左右欄中各有單複數的句子，先聽錄音帶唸一次，分辨是單數句子還是複數句子，然後再重複一次加深印象：

1. A guide leads tourists.	Guides lead tourists.
2. A student attends classes.	Students attend classes.
3. Boys like sports.	A boy likes sports.
4. Secretaries type letters.	A secretary types letters.
5. A singer records songs.	Singers record songs.
6. A student needs textbooks.	Students need textbooks.
7. A reporter writes articles.	Reporters write articles.

8. Americans understand English.   An American understands English.

9. Children love pictures.   A child loves pictures.

10. Singers sing songs.   A singer sings songs.

11. Teachers teach students.   A teacher teaches students.

12. A tourist visits places.   Tourists visit places.

13. Students read books.   A student reads books.

14. Dogs eat bones.   A dog eats bones.

15. A bank lends money.   Banks lend money.

16. A bookcase contains books.   Bookcases contain books.

17. A student studies problems.   Students study problems.

≪ **Coffee Break** ≫

What are four seasons ?

→ *The four seasons are pepper, salt, vinegar, and mustard.*

四季是什麼？

→ 四季是胡椒、鹽、醋，和芥末。

✦ season 是「季節」，也是「調味料」的意思。您可曾想過four seasons 不是 spring, summer, autumn, and winter, 而是 pepper, salt, vinegar, and mustard 簡直有天壤之別呢！

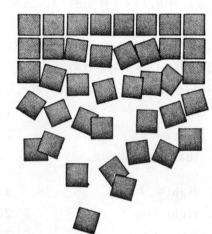

LESSON 20

本課提供更多特殊的發音問題，以資
參考。

20 ① /t/ 置於不同位置的發音方式

1. get 中的 /t/：字尾的 /t/ 通常不吐氣。

2. get down 中的 /t/：/t/ 在另一個子音之前，發音時也不吐氣。

3. get a book 中的 /t/：/t/ 置於兩個母音之間，發音時只要舌頭輕拍一下上齒齦就可以了。

仔細聽以下各組例子的發音，就可以體會出其中的差異。請跟著唸一次：

1. that	1. get
2. that way	2. get some stamps
3. that apple	3. getting some stamps
1. right	1. eat
2. right now	2. eat two apples
3. right away	3. eat an orange
1. white	1. wait
2. the white one	2. wait for me
3. the white album	3. waiting for me
1. No, I'm not.	1. Was it ?
2. No, I'm not coming.	2. Was it there ?
3. No, I'm not a teacher.	3. Was it a good idea ?
1. This is it.	1. They often meet.
2. Here it comes.	2. They often meet John.
3. Here it is.	3. They're meeting John.
1. visit	1. He sat.
2. I visit them.	2. He sat down.
3. I visited them.	3. Saturday

20 ② on the 中 /nð/ 的發音

/nð/ 的位置圖　　　　　　　　/n/ 的位置圖

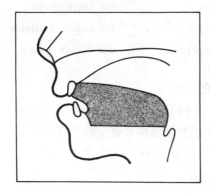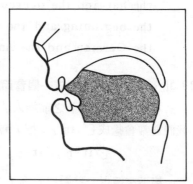

　　發 /n/ 時，舌頭在上齒齦的位置。但是當 /n/ 位於 /ð/ 之前，如 in the，on the，舌頭只需抵住上齒內側即可。請做以下練習：

　　　　1. 〔ɪnðə, ɪnðə, ɪnðə, ɪnðə …〕= in the
　　　　2. 〔ɑnðə, ɑnðə, ɑnðə, ɑnðə …〕= on the
　　　　3. 〔ənðə, ənðə, ənðə, ənðə …〕= and the

　　請練習以下這些包含 /nð/ 常見的片語：

1. 〔ɪnðə〕
　　in the class
　　in the car
　　in the park
　　in the morning

2. 〔ɪnði〕
　　in the office
　　in the afternoon
　　in the U.S.
　　in the English book

3. 〔ɑnðə〕
　　on the table
　　on the bus
　　on the train
　　on the first floor

4. 〔ənðə〕
　　the book and the pencil
　　the boy and the girl
　　the bus and the taxi
　　the teacher and the student

5. 〔əði〕

　　the orange and the apple

　　the hat and the overcoat

　　the beginning and the end

　　the German and the American

6. 其他

　　in this hospital

　　on that desk

　　in these houses

　　on those days

20③ eaten 中獨自組成一個音節的 / n̩ /

　　在 eaten 的 / n / 之前插入 / ə / 的音，唸成〔'itən〕並非錯誤，但是我們通常會唸成〔'itn̩〕，把 / n / 這個音唸得很輕。請反覆練習：

$$〔'it-n̩ , 'it-n̩ , 'it-n̩ , 'it-n̩ ... 〕$$

　　接下來練習一些類似的例子：

1. cert*ain*　　　2. cert*ain*ly　　　3. stud*ent*

4. import*ant*　　5. did*n*'t　　　6. less*on*

7. list*en*　　　8. is*n*'t　　　9. was*n*'t

　　以下這些片語與句子中的 and 也發成 / n̩ /：

1. Mr. *and* Mrs.　　　　2. Bill *and* Ken

3. cats *and* dogs　　　　4. pens *and* pencils

5. Mr. and Mrs. Walton didn't come.

6. He certainly is important.

7. The student isn't listening.

20④ little 中的 / l̩ /

　　little 中的第二個 / l / 自成一個音節，帶有母音的性質，所以發 / t / 時，只要舌頭輕拍一下上齒齦就可以了（即 20① 第三種 / t / 的發音法）。請反覆練習：

$$〔'lɪt-l̩ , 'lɪt-l̩ , 'lɪt-l̩ , 'lɪt-l̩ ... 〕$$

　　接下來練習一些類似的例子：

1. midd*le*　　2. tot*al*　　3. bott*le*　　4. Mr. Rand*le*

再把這些字帶入句中練習：

1. He's a little too tall.
2. The total is eight.
3. It's in the middle of the room.
4. Mr. Randle drank two bottles.

20 ⑤ can 及 can't 的發音

請注意以下四點：

1. can 重讀時唸成〔 kæn 〕。
2. can 非重讀時唸成〔 kən 〕或〔 kn̩ 〕
3. 句尾 can't〔 kænt 〕中的 / t / 吐氣。
4. can't 後接子音時，/ t / 不吐氣。

把上述四項帶入句中練習：

1. Yes, I ′can.〔 kæn 〕
2. I ′can go.〔 kn̩ 〕
3. No, I ′can't.〔 kænt 〕
4. I ′can't go.〔 kænt 〕

現在練習以下各例句中 can 及 can't 的用法：

（a）代換

	They can speak English very well.〔 kn̩ 〕
I	I can speak English very well.　〔 kn̩ 〕
can't	I can't speak English very well.　〔 kænt 〕

繼續以下的練習：

1. we — We can't speak English very well.
2. Bob — Bob can't speak English very well.
3. can — Bob can speak English very well.
4. Tom — Tom can speak English very well.
5. she — She can speak English very well.
6. can't — She can't speak English very well.
7. John — John can't speak English very well.
8. they — They can't speak English very well.
9. can — They can speak English very well.
10. I — I can speak English very well.

(b) 簡答中的 can 及 can't

	Yes, he can.	〔kæn〕
they	Yes, they can.	
no	No, they can't.	〔kænt〕

繼續以下的練習：

1. we	2. you	3. yes	4. she
5. I	6. no	7. he	8. they
9. yes	10. we	11. you	12. no
13. she	14. I	15. yes	16. you

≪ Coffee Break ≫

Why is your nose in the middle of your face？

→ *Because it is a scenter.*

　爲什麼你的鼻子在臉的中央？

→ 因爲它是個嗅覺的器官。

✦ *scenter* 〔'sɛntɚ〕（嗅覺器官）與 *center*（中心）讀音相同，而鼻子本來就是生在臉的中央。

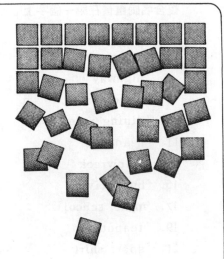

LESSON 21

本課主要介紹字羣的重音。先從複合名詞的重音開始,對幾種常見的字羣重音作次第的介紹,其中並包括名字、數字、分數、小數、錢和地址的重音。

21 ① 字群的重音

複合名詞重音在第一個字上。（重音記號〔 ' 〕）

例：
1. 'classroom
2. 'blackboard
3. 'milkman
4. 'railroad
5. 'highway
6. 'grape juice
7. 'armchair
8. 'toothache
9. 'dining room
10. 'football
11. 'headache
12. 'fire engine
13. 'shipwreck
14. 'high school
15. 'bus driver
16. 'headache
17. 'night school
18. 'grocery store
19. 'teapot
20. 'breadbasket
21. 'sport shirt
22. 'swimming practice
23. 'flower garden
24. 'train conductor
25. 'news reporter
26. 'piano store
27. dis'cussion group
28. 'coffee shop
29. 'candy shop
30. 'football
31. 'bathing suit
32. 'fencing mask
33. 'golf club
34. 'police department
35. vo'cational school
36. 'television set
37. 'library book
38. 'history professor
39. de'tective story
40. 'movie star

21 ② 下列句子中含有複合名詞，記住複合名詞的重音在第一個字上。請跟著唸，並看看複合字是怎樣形成的：

1. A *store* which sells *furniture* is a *'furniture store*
2. A *train* which carries *passengers* is a *'passenger train*.
3. A *store* which sells *candy* is a *'candy store*.
4. *Juice* made from *tomatoes* is called *'tomato juice*.
5. A *box* in which you keep *bread* is called a *'breadbox*.

21 ③ 所有格＋名詞，重音在名詞上。

例： 1. my 'name 　　2. my 'friend
　　 3. our pro'fessor 　　4. your 'birthday
　　 5. her 'flower garden 　6. my 'notebook
　　 7. his 'watch 　　8. their 'car
　　 9. my 'teacher 　　10. our 'high school

冠詞 a, an, the, some ＋名詞，重音在名詞上。

例： 1. a 'pen 　　2. an 'egg
　　 3. a 'table 　　4. an 'animal
　　 5. the 'paper 　　6. some 'fruit
　　 7. a 'machine 　　8. a to'mato
　　 9. the 'bus driver 　　10. the popu'lation

21 ④ 介系詞＋名詞，重音在名詞上。

例： 1. by 'bus 　　2. by 'car
　　 3. by 'train 　　4. for 'Helen
　　 5. with 'Mary 　　6. at 'home
　　 7. at 'work 　　8. in 'class
　　 9. at 'play 　　10. on 'time

介系詞＋冠詞＋名詞，重音在名詞上。

例： 1. on the 'bus 　　2. in the 'room
　　 3. in a 'minute 　　4. for the 'teacher
　　 5. at the 'store 　　6. in the 'wintertime

21 ⑤ 形容詞＋名詞，重音在名詞上。

例： 1. good 'movie 　　2. good 'mother
　　 3. rich 'men 　　4. hard 'worker
　　 5. brown 'sweater 　　6. black um'brella

7. white ′elephant	8. ten ′bears
9. good a′bility	10. cloudy ′day
11. exciting ′movie	12. hungry ′animal

名詞與分詞也可修飾名詞，重音在被修飾的名詞上。

例：
1. fried ′eggs	2. falling ′snow
3. wool ′suit	4. broken ′leg
5. winter ′rain	6. spring ′weather
7. glass ′window	8. singing ′bird

21 ⑥ 動詞＋副詞，重音在副詞上。

例：
1. go ′quickly	2. try it a′gain
3. do it a′gain	4. come ′here
5. go ′there	

頻率副詞＋動詞，重音在動詞上

例：
1. always ′plays	2. usually ′came
3. often ′comes	4. sometimes ′helps
5. generally ′find	

21 ⑦ 名詞前有兩個形容詞時，重音在名詞。二個形容詞都是次重音。

例：
1. eight new ′students	2. big white ′suitcase
3. a funny old ′man	4. a new black ′car
5. a beautiful white ′bird	6. a big tall ′tree

動詞（＋代名詞）＋介副詞，重音在介副詞。

例：
1. put ′on	2. turn ′over
3. think ′over	4. put it ′on
5. turn it ′over	6. put them ′away

21 8 **姓名的重音在姓上**。

例： 1. John 'Brown   2. Helen 'Black

     3. Betty 'White   4. Bill 'Smith

     5. Roger Henry 'Jones   6. A. A. 'Fair

數字的重音常在最後一個字上。

例： 1. *555*   five hundred (and) fifty-'five

     2. *102*   one hundred (and) 'two

     3. *1111*   one 'thousand, one hundred and 'eleven

     4. *51929*   fifty-one 'thousand, nine hundred twenty-'nine

     5. *348999*   three hundred forty-eight 'thousand, nine hundred ninety-'nine

21 9 **分數的重音**在最後一個字上。

例： 1. $12\frac{1}{5}$ twelve and one 'fifth *or* twelve and a 'fifth

     2. $13\frac{1}{2}$ thirteen and a 'half

     3. $18\frac{3}{8}$ eighteen and three-'eighths

     4. $19\frac{5}{9}$ nineteen and five-'ninths

含小數重音也在最後一個字上。

例： 1. *14.5*   fourteen and a 'half

                  fourteen and five-'tenths

                  fourteen point 'five

     2. *28.1*   twenty-eight and one-'tenth

                  twenty-eight point 'one

     3. *1.7*   one point 'seven

     4. *1.02*   one and two 'hundredths

     5. *7.1*   seven point 'one

21 ⑩ **錢的重音**視數目多寡而有不同，原則上是最後一個字上，或說時停頓的那個字上。

例：1. $ 4.26 four dollars and twenty-six 'cents
       four twenty-'six

  2. $. 326.00 three hundred twenty-six 'dollars
       three twenty-'six

  3. $ 101.01 one hundred and one dollars and one 'cent

  4. $ 2,230.65 two 'thousand, two hundred thirty 'dollars
       and sixty-five 'cents

地址的重音

在美國，一個地址常包括(1)號碼，(2)街道名，(3)城市，(4)州。
如果地址中有道（avenue），巷（lane）或路（road），重音常在這些字上。

例：1. 321 Maple Avenue
   three twenty-one Maple 'Avenue

  2. 1600 Pennsylvania Avenue
   sixteen hundred Pennsylvania 'Avenue

  3. 1500 Cherry Lane
   fifteen hundred Cherry 'Lane

  4. 818 Riggs Road
   eight eighteen Riggs 'Road

如果地址中含有街（street），重音常在 street 前面一個字。

例：1. 1500 Cherry Street
   fifteen hundred 'Cherry Street

  2. 800 Carlton Street
   eight hundred 'Carlton Street

3. 1313　16th St.

　　　thirteen　thirteen　Sixteenth　Street

4. 400　Main St.

　　　four hundred ′Main Street

　　如果是完整的地址，常分爲二段說，前段包括號碼和街道，後段包括城市和州名。二段各有重音，請唸下面例子：

例：1. 512　Cherry　Lane，Denver，Colorado

　　　　　　　five　twelve　Cherry ′Lane，Denver，Colo′rado

　　　2. 314　Maple　Avenue，Atlanta，Georgia

　　　　　　　three fourteen Maple 　′Avenue，Atlanta，′Georgia

　　　3. 2332 Ross　Street，Buffalo，New York

　　　　　　　twenty-three thirty-two ′Ross Street，Buffalo，

　　　　　New ′York

《 **Coffee Break** 》

Why should taxicab drivers be brave men ?

→ *Because "none but the brave deserve the fair."*

　爲什麼計程車司機應該是勇敢的人呢？

→因爲「只有勇者才配得佳人。」

　　✦計程車司機靠計程車的車費維生，車費是 *fare* 〔fɛr〕讀起來不是和 *fair* （美人）一模一樣嗎？所以如果計程車司機不勇敢的話，怎能得到 " fare " 呢？

〜〜〜〜〜〜〜〜〜 **Tongue   Trippers 繞口令** 〜〜〜〜〜〜〜〜〜

THE Leith police dismisseth us,

I'm thankful, sir, to say ;

The Leith police dismisseth us,

They thought we sought to stay.

The Leith police dismisseth us,

We both sighed sighs apiece,

And the sigh that we sighed as we said

goodbye

Was the size of the Leith police.

萊斯警察把我們放了，

我得說，先生，我很感激；

萊斯警察把我們放了，

他們以爲我們想留下。

萊斯警察把我們放了，

我們雙方都各自嘆氣，

當我們說再見時嘆的氣

和萊斯警察的體型一般大。

dismiss〔dɪsˊmɪs〕*v.* 釋放；解散

sought〔sɔt〕*v.*（seek的過去式）試圖；企圖；想

sigh〔saɪ〕*v., n.* 嘆息　　apiece〔əˊpis〕*adv.* 各個；每個

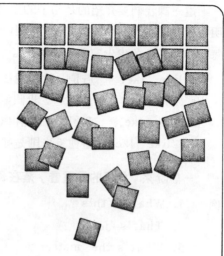

LESSON 22

本課介紹句子的重音。先從一般句子的重音介紹起，再列舉一些例外的情形，並加上練習。

22 ① 句子的重音

　　這一課我們要介紹的是句子的重音。下面列舉一些基本的規則加以說明；但是同一句話會因所代表的意思不同，而使重音位置產生變化，因此每一項規則多多少少有例外的情形。例如：

We like ′Ike. 　　這是一般的說法。意思是：Ike 是我們喜歡的人。

We ′like Ike. 　　意思是：我們並不討厭 Ike。

′We like Ike. 　　意思是：或許你不喜歡他，可是我們喜歡 Ike。

′We ′like ′Ike！ 這種說法則是喊叫式的口號。

　　一般說來，**句子的最重音，落在倒數第一個強讀字上**。

例：　1. What's ′this？　　　　2. It's a ′pen.

　　　3. That's ′John.　　　　4. He's a ′doctor.

　　　5. What's the ′matter？　6. He's a ′milkman.

　　　7. I have to buy some toothpaste.

　　　8. Is he ′bicycling？

　　　9. It was a ′grammar book.

　　10. It was a cloudy ′day.　11. We saw a good ′movie.

　　12. She can't come at nine o'clock.

　　13. The sweater was ′beautiful.

　　14. The newspaper hasn't ′come.

　　15. She's wearing a cotton ′dress.

　　16. Your book is on the ′desk.

　　17. I thought it was very ′nice.

　　18. The movie was extremely ′good.

　　19. Miss Johnson is sometimes ′cross.

　　20. He started ′counting it.

　　21. The Smiths fixed up their ′house.

　　22. She put away her ′clothes.

　　23. This safe doesn't have a ′lock on it.

註：強讀字爲<u>名詞</u>、<u>動詞</u>（含動狀詞）、<u>形容詞</u>、<u>副詞</u>、<u>感嘆詞</u>、<u>指示代名詞</u>、<u>所有格代名詞</u>、<u>介副詞</u>。

22 ② 附加問句、簡答句重音在助動詞或 be 動詞上。

例： 1. He won't ʹdo it, ʹwill he？ No, he ʹwon't.

2. You can ʹdo it, ʹcan't you？ Yes, I ʹcan.

3. You were ʹtrying, ʹweren't you？ Yes, I ʹwas.

4. Mrs. White accepted the inviʹtation, ʹdidn't she？

5. You can hear the ʹspeaker, ʹcan't you？

6. You want the ʹbiggest one, ʹdon't you？

7. It didn't ʹhurt, ʹdid it？

8. You like playing the ʹpiano, ʹdon't you？

9. You can ʹcome, ʹcan't you, Mrs. ʹChase？

10. You'd like to ʹgo, ʹwouldn't you, Mrs. ʹHouse？

22 ③ 主要子句＋副詞子句，二個子句分別有重音。

例： 1. He went to ʹbed after they ʹleft.

2. I had finished all my ʹwork before the clock struck ʹten.

3. They ʹdid it because they ʹhad to.

4. We went to ʹbed after they ʹleft.

5. You'd better wear ʹgloves when you go ʹskiing.

6. Mrs. Jones listens to the ʹradio while she gets ʹdinner.

7. After they ʹdanced, they were ʹtired.

8. If I had ʹmoney, I'd ʹtravel.

9. Until it ʹrains, it will be ʹdusty.

10. If you are going to ʹdo it, do it ʹnow.

22 ④ 如果一個子句中同樣重要的強讀字不只一個，則它們都是重音所在。

例： 1. I got my car ʹoiled, ʹgreased and reʹpaired.

2. I'd like some ʹcereal, ʹcoffee and ʹjuice.

3. All he does is ʹsleep, ʹeat and ʹplay.

4. I'd like some 'bacon, 'eggs and 'toast.

5. Do you want po'tatoes or 'rice ?

6. Did you 'see her or 'talk to her ?

7. Was she 'happy or 'sad ?

8. Would you like 'coffee or 'milk ?

9. Is it 'sunny or 'cloudy ?

10. Did you talk to 'John or 'Bill ?

11. Do you like 'music, or 'art, or 'drama ?

12. Does he like 'swimming, or 'boating, or 'ice skat-ing ?

13. Do you think it's going to 'rain, 'snow, or 'sleet ?

14. Do you need any 'shirts, or 'socks, or 'ties ?

15. Would you like 'orange juice, to'mato juice, or 'pineapple juice ?

22 5 練習 請跟著讀下列的對話，並注意字上標示的重音記號。

Salesman: Good 'morning, 'sir. May I 'help you ?

Customer : 'Yes. I need some 'shirts.

Salesman: What size do you 'take ?

Customer : Fifteen-thirty-'four.

Salesman: Any particular 'color ?

Customer : 'Yes. I want one 'white shirt and one 'blue one.

再讀下列的練習：

John : Did you see the 'baseball game Sunday ?

Henry: 'Yes. It was exciting, 'wasn't it ?

John : It sure 'was. I'm glad we 'won.

Henry: Here's 'Ted's house. Maybe 'he'd like to play.

John : All 'right. 'Call him.

Henry: 'Ted. 'Ted.

22 ⑥ 凡是**句子前後文意對比或强調的，重音落在强調或對比上**。

例： 1. Jim can 'swim, but he can't 'dive.

2. I ate the 'food, but I wasn't 'hungry.

3. He lives in New 'York and works at the United 'Nations.

4. I made an apˈpointment, but I didn't 'keep it.

5. I drove the 'car, but I was 'careful.

6. He leaves at 'nine, and returns at 'five.

7. It wasn't 'easy, but I 'did it.

8. We saw the 'movie, but we didn't 'like it.

9. He wrote the 'letter, but he never 'mailed it.

10. We went to the 'meeting, and had a good 'time.

22 ⑦ 練習

1. Are you calling 'Bill ?

2. Are you 'calling, 'Bill ?

3. May I help you with your 'coat,

| 'John ? |
| Mr. 'Smith ? |
| Mrs. 'Green ? |
| 'sir ? |

4. Did you 'see it, 'Jeff ?

5. Will you do a 'favor for me ?

22 ⑧ 在比較的句子中，重音在 as 或 than 後的（代）名詞上。

例： 1. This is better than 'that.

2. John is taller than 'Bill.

3. Milk is better than 'tea.

4. Japanese is more difficult than 'English.

5. This one is better than 'that one.

6. She is as pretty as a 'picture.

    7. She's as happy as a 'lark.

    8. He's as sly as a 'fox.

    9. It's as easy as 'pie.

  10. It's as heavy as 'lead.

22 ⑨ 問答練習

1. Did he buy a 'car ? Yes. He bought a 'black one.

2. Which one did you 'buy ? I bought the ex'pensive one.

3. Is that a good 'book ? Yes. It's a very a'musing one.

4. Which one do you 'want ? I want the 'best one.

5. Are you going to the 'party ? Yes. It's a very im'portant one.

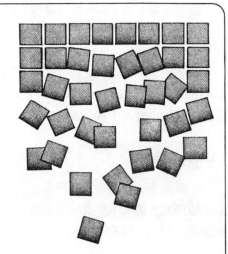

LESSON 23

本課告訴您何謂意羣（ thought group ），介紹意羣的種類，並加上練習。

23 ① 意群（ The Thought Group ）

意群是決定英文節奏與流暢的單位。

學習意群最主要是爲了體會英文的節奏與流暢感，幫助自己聽懂英文，說流利的英文。

我們說英文或讀英文時，常一口氣說幾個字，就像讀 "constitutional" 或 "everlasting" 這樣的長字一樣。說或讀得告一段落便稍微停頓，以使人了解，這種文字的段落，就叫做「意群」。

23 ② 意群的種類

一般說來，意群可分二類：

(a) **短而完整的句子**形成一個意群。這種意群常包括一個簡單的主詞、一個動詞、和一個簡單的受詞或補語。

請練習下列的句子，句子（ ′ ）的字，應該重讀：

1. He gave me ten 'dollars.
2. How ćold it is !
3. Why are you in 'town ?
4. Don't be 'late.
5. Are you having a good 'time ?
6. The 'snow was falling.
7. She's very 'pretty.
8. The cost of living has gone 'up.

(b) 另一類是**長句中的部分**形成意群。這類意群可能包括以下部分：

1. 主詞和它的修飾語。
2. 動詞和副詞（ 片語 ）。
3. 從屬子句。
4. 介詞片語。

23 ③ 長句中意群的練習

　　下列的長句都已經被分成意群。每個意群中，有一個字上面標有（′）記號，應該重讀；每句裏有一個字下面劃底線，是句中讀的時候應該最強調的字。

　　請跟著唸下面的句子。唸的時候，不但要注意意群，還要注意重音：

1. If you want to ′get there / before the ′curtain goes up, / you'd better take a ′<u>taxi</u>. /

2. After he took his ′bath, / he dressed in a ′hurry, / ran to catch the ′bus, / and got to his ap′pointment / before it was too ′<u>late</u>. /

3. Last ′winter, / she told me she was going to learn to ′<u>ski</u> / if she could find a ′teacher / who was very ′handsome. /

4. The President of the United ′States / took a short va′<u>cation</u> / after he had won the e′lection / by a large ma′jority. /

5. The ′<u>weather</u>-man reports / that there will be ′snow tonight, / with high ′winds / and a considerable drop in ′temperature. /

6. On the way to New ′York / he stopped over in ′<u>Rome,</u> / where he visited some ′friends / who had been living in ′Italy / for the past three ′years. /

7. ′<u>Some</u> people / like their coffee ′strong, / with lots of ′sugar in it / and without ′cream. / ′<u>Others</u> prefer it / ′not so strong / and put ′both cream and sugar in it. /

8. If World War ′Ⅲ should come, / there would be great ′danger / to ′all the people of the ′world / because of the ′fall-out / from the explosion of atomic ′<u>bombs</u>. /

9. Reading a'loud / is 'excellent practice / for learning the 'rhythm of a language, / after you have learned 'something / about the way to link words to'gether, / to give to "im'portant words" / their proper stress and 'pitch, / and to reduce the 'vowels / of "unim'portant words." /

10. Practice in reading a'loud / will help you to recognize 'thought groups ; / but it is better to read 'silently / when you want to read 'fast. /

注意：不是所有的人都把長句子分成一樣的意群。說話快的人有時把二、三個意群併成一個。但初學的人最好先練習短的意群，熟練以後，再練習長的。

23 ④ 下面有二個練習，都已經被分成意群。請跟著唸，並注意重音：

(a) English in Paris

If you ever go to 'Paris, / you will find it's very 'easy / to make your way around 'town, / if you speak 'English fairly well. / Most of the 'taxi drivers, / the ho'tel clerks, / and the 'waiters / in the well-known 'restaurants / speak 'English. / In the big de'partment stores, / and in most of the small 'shops, / in the 'center of the city, / there is usually a 'clerk / who can help you find what you 'want, / if you ask for it in 'English. /

On the 'buses, / in the 'subway, / or just walking around the 'streets, / you can generally ask directions from 'anyone / in 'English, / and get some 'help, / if you are in 'trouble, / or have lost your 'way. /

'French people, / the 'young ones especially, / like to 'practice their English. / 'Most of them / have studied it in 'school, / sometimes for eight or ten 'years, / and it's

always 'pleasant / to find an opportunity to 'talk a foreign
language / you have worked long and 'hard to acquire· /

And don't forget the gen'darmes (the po'lice) . / 'Most
of them / know some 'English. / There are so 'many /
English- speaking 'tourists in Paris, / that a po'liceman / has
to be able to talk 'enough English, / to give directions and
information when asked. / Of 'course / he may on oc'casion/
be obliged to arr'est some English- speaking people, / 'too, /
if they violate 'traffic laws, / have a 'car accident, / or
even do something 'worse. /

A knowledge of 'English / can be a big 'help to a
tourist / in 'any part of the world. /

(b) 下面這個練習裏，有些字上標有次重音 (″) 請跟著讀, 注意重音：

Phoning for an Appointment

Albert : Hel'lo, / is this the 'Andersons' 'residence ? /

Voice : 'Yes, / 'this is the ″Andersons'. / who do you wish
to 'speak to ? /

Albert : I'd like to speak to Professor 'Anderson, /″please, /
if he's there. / I've been trying to find him at the
'college, / but there was no one in his 'office. /

Voice : I think he's here 'somewhere. / Just hold the 'line a
moment, / and I'll 'call him. /

········· After a short wait ·········

Professor A : 'Hello, / this is Pro″fessor 'Anderson speaking . /

Albert : Oh, hel'lo, / Pro″fessor ″Anderson. / This is Albert
'Black. / I'm sorry to bother you at 'home, /

″sir, / but I need to ′talk to you, / and I've tried to reach you at your ′office, / three or ′four times, / in the last few ′days. /

Professor A : I'm sorry you couldn't ′find me ; / I've been so ′busy / with special com′mittee meetings, / that I haven't kept my ′office hours / the way I ′should. / What is it you ′want, / ′Albert ? /

Albert : It's about my ′term paper. / You told me to ′talk to you about it / before the end of the ′week. / Tomorrow's ′Friday, / and I have to leave ′town Saturday morning, / to take care of some ′business for my ′father. /

Professor A : I'll be at my office at three-′thirty tomorrow. / Are you ′free ′then, / or do you have a ′class ? /

Albert : I have a ′lab / from two to ′five on Fridays. /

Professor A : How about the ′morning ? / I could see you at ten ′thirty. / I'm free until e′leven. /

Albert : That's just ′fine ! / I can ′make it then. /

Professor A : All ′right then. / I'll see you in my ′office. /

Albert : Thanks a ′lot, / Pro″fessor. / It's very ′kind of you. /

•••••••• 學習出版,天天進步 ••••••••

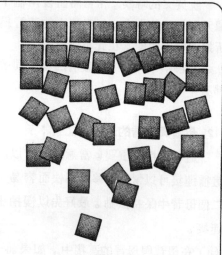

LESSON 24

本課作連音的介紹。告訴您何謂連音，
以及連音的方式。

24① 連音

說英文的時候，常常將前後兩個字連在一起唸，這樣就形成連音。本單元所討論的內容，以意群中的連音為主；意群與意群之間因為稍有停頓，所以連音不明顯，在此不予討論。

意群中字與字的連接有四種不同的情形，每一種對意群的節奏與流暢都有不同的影響。

24② 母音與母音的連接（記號：y̆ w̆）

這種連接很重要。當意群中，以母音結尾的字接著以母音開頭的字時，這種連接可以幫助字移動得快而容易。但是這需要長時間練習，使聲帶在二個母音中保持振動。最好先以慢拍子、低音調，及誇張的力量練習這種連接。

(a) 在母音與母音的連接中，如果前一個母音發音的時候形成於口腔的前部，如 /ɪ/、/i/、/e/（參考第十二課），就以 you 中的滑音 /j/ 來連接它及後面的母音。以記號〔y〕標示。如：

> May I; she isn't; high up; they eat; pie or cake;
>   y   y   y   y   y
>
> very easy。
>   y

(b) 如果前一個母音發音時形成於口腔的後部，如 /u/、/ʊ/、/o/，就以 we 中的滑音 /w/ 來連接它及下一個母音。以記號〔w〕標示。如：

> How I; you expect; do it; to us; know it; blue or red。
>   w   w   w   w   w   w

注意：有些時候一個字裏母音與母音也以滑音來連接。例：

> a'greeable, 'doing, aorta, 'Noel, pro(h)ibition, reality,
>   y   w   y   w   w   y
>
> Seattle, San Diego, coexist, cooperate, coeducation。
>   y   y   w   w   w

另外，如果第一個母音的字母是 -a，發輕音的 /ə/，就沒有滑音，但聲帶保持振動。如：

Virginia 'answers ; the 'opera "ended ; a 'sofa in the
ə　　　　　　　　　ə　　　　　　　　ə

"room ; 'Iowa is "near "Missouri 。
　　　　　ə

練習：

1. We 'always "say it "that "way.
　　y　　　　　y

They "go 'in and "go 'out.
　　w　　　　　w

2. "May I "see another one ?
　　y　　y

She's "too 'old to "ask "that.
　　　w　　　　w

3. They are 'free as "birds.
　　y

You appear "now and 'then.
　w　　　　w

4. He "under"stands the 'answer.
　　y　　　　　y

Do our "friends 'know it ?
　w　　　　　w

5. She is 'happy in "Logan.
　　y　　　y

You "ought to "speak to 'everyone.
　w　　　　　　w

6. The "end of the 'evening has come.
　　y　　　　　y

"Two and "two are "four.
　　w　　　w

7. They "eat "many 'other "things.
　　y　　y

So I "go "into a 'store.
　w　　w　　w

8. They "say 'I "ate the "apples.
   _y   _y   _y

   So "all of you "others can "come.
   _w   _w   _ə

9. "Pay us for the "other 'ticket.
   _y   _y

   No 'other "show is "so 'interesting.
   _w   _w   _w

10. It will be "over "three or 'four.
    _y   _y

    "Send a 'blue one to 'everyone.
    _w   _w

11. You can 'fly over the 'Alps.
    _y   _y

    They "flew "over "two "old 'towns.
    _w   _w

12. 'High in the 'sky are some 'birds.
    _y   _y   _ə

    Who "asked 'you a "question ?
    _w   _w

13. 'Thirty of my "answers are correct.
    _y   _y

    "How and " now are 'adverbs.
    _w   _w

14. I "only "want my 'own.
    _y   _y

    You "either 'go or 'stay.
    _w   _w

15. Can she "ever 'see it ?
    _y   _y

    How 'old were you in 'May ?
    _w   _w

16. The ″Rey of ′Tunis ″may arrive.
        y   y

   He ″talked to us ″too ′often.
           w   w

24 ③ 子音與母音的連接（記號：‿）

子音與子音的連接，會阻礙意群中聲音的流暢。如：Take that back.
但子音與母音的連接却幫助了音的流暢。如：Out of an old opera.

字尾 e 在大多數的字中是無聲的。連接時要連接 e 前的子音。

練習：

1. At a ′store ; at another ″store ; at an old ″store ;
   at an ″old ′empty ″store.

2. From an ′aunt ; from an ′aunt of ″mine ; from an ″old
   ′aunt of ″mine ; from another ″old ″aunt of ″mine.

3. For an ′hour ; for another ″hour ; for another ″hour
   and a ′half.

4. With our ′uncle ; with our ″Uncl(e) ′Edward ; with
   another of our ″Uncles.

5. The name of a ′restaurant ; the ″names of our ′restau-
   rants ; the ″names of ′any of ″our ″restaurants in ′town.

6. As I was ′entering ; as I was ′eating ; as I was ″eating
   at an ″interesting ″old ′restaurant.

7. To ″tak(e) a ′shower ; he ′wanted a ″shower ; he ″wanted
   a ″shower in an extra ″big ′hurry.

8. ″Most of us ; ′most of us in our ″class ; ′most of us in our ″class ar(e) ′interested ; ′most of us in our ″class ar(e) ″interested in ″answering ″out ′loud.

9. About a ′year a͞go ; he ″cam(e) about a ′year a͞go ; she ″said (h)e ″cam(e) about a ′year a͞go ″last ′August.

10. ″After ′Ellen arrives ; ″eat ″after ′Ellen arrives ; they ″say we'll ″eat ″after ′Ellen arrives in ″town.

11. In an ″old ″automobile ; they ″rod(e) in an ″old ″automobile ; ″they ″rod(e) around a͞whil(e) in an ″old ″automobile.

12. ″Lik(e) ″our ′own ; ″lik(e) our ′own ″accent ; he ″has an ″accent as unusual as our ′own ″accent.

再練習子音與母音的連接。先標出連接的記號◡，再跟著讀。

Class Reunion

About a week ago, I was at a party with a lot of officers of our senior class, which graduated in 1947. It was held in the evening at a late hour, so that we could all make it. A number of our old classmates had an engagement earlier in the evening for a dinner of the Alumni Association, so they couldn't get away for an eight-thirty event.

When it got around to nine o'clock, and they hadn't showed up yet, we went ahead anyway. There wasn't any

time to waste in waiting for the late ones, so we started
our program on the dot. It only took a few minutes to get
organized, and all of us pitched in to make it a real old-
time celebration. There were toasts and speeches, and a
lot of tom-foolery, in addition to the more serious business
of doing honor to the leader of our class, which had made
such an excellent record in the late forties.

24 ④ 母音與子音的連接 (記號 -)

英語中以母音結尾的字比例不多。但有些短字，多半是單音節，以母
音結尾，常用在會話中。如：The, a, I, me, you, he, she, we, they,
to, into, so, though, through, how, now, may, my, by, any,
new, few, blue, true, free , high, low, tree, sea, tea, be, see,
do, go, know, grow, show, row, throw, sew。

這些短字在意群中常一個接一個。如果說的時候不加重，便說得很快。
有些意群裏，可以找到二或三，或多至十個這樣的字連在一起。注意聽別
人對話時用到的這種短字群，熟悉以後，自己也能輕鬆愉快地加入對話。

練習

1. The-ˊmovies； to-the-ˊmovies；"go-to-the-ˊmovies；to-"go-
   to-the-ˊmovies；you-do-"go-to-the-"movies，"don't ˊyou？

2. The-ˊgame；to-the-ˊgame；"go-to-the-ˊgame；to-"go-to-
   the-ˊgame；do-ˊyou-"go-to-the-ˊgame？

3. The-ˊbarber "shop；to-the-ˊbarber "shop；"go-to-the-ˊnew-
   "barber "shop；do-you-"go-to-the-ˊnew-barber ˊshop？

4. "Blue-ˊshirt；a-"blue-ˊshirt；a-"new-"blue-ˊshirt；"buy a-
   "new-"blue-ˊshirt；I-"saw-you "buy a-"new-"blue-ˊshirt；
   I-"saw-you-"buy-the-"new-"blue-ˊshirt you-"have "on.

5. ′How-″do-you ; ″how-″do-you-′do ? ; ″how-do-you-
   ′know-″why-they-″do ″that ?

6. ″Now-we-″go-to-the-′show ; ″now-we-″go-to-the-′new-
   ″show-to-″see-the-″Blue-′Dragon .

7. ″So-you-′see ; ″so-you-″see-′how ; ″so-you-″see-″how-
   ′few-we-″now-′have .

8. We-′see ; we-′do-″see ; we-′do-″see-″why ; ″so-we-′do-
   ″see-″why ; so-we-′do-″see-″why-they-″know-″how-to-
   ″grow-′flowers .

9. They-″show-″you ; they-′show-″you-′how ; they-″show-
   you-″how-to-′do ; they-″show-you-″how-to-″do-the-
   ″two-″new-′dance ″steps .

10. ′Why-″do-you ; ″why-″do-you-′try ; why-do-you-″try-
    to-″be-′through-″by-″two-to-″three-′minutes be″fore
    I-′go ?

再做一個練習。下面有一段文章，請用（-）記號連接子音前，以母音
結尾的短字。讀的時候，儘量讀得快而順暢。

Where and How to Go

So now you want to know how to do the sights in New
York ? You don't need to be too rich to see the high spots.
When I say the high spots, I know you may be thinking of the
hot spots. But you may do so many ′interesting things at
small cost, if you don't try to do the hot spots.

If you know how to use the subway to go to where you

want, you may be sure you will save a lot of money. To go
in a taxi to see the high spots, the cost may be too high.
Do you see the point?

A true New Yorker knows how to go to ″Coney ′Island,
how to go to the Statue of Libery, how to go to the Zoo,
how to get to the ″Empire ′State ″Building, to the mu′seums,
to the United Nations, by taking the subway.

I may have some time this afternoon to show you the
two new bank buildings near the ″Grand ′Central, if you
want to see how they look. Maybe we can do a few other
sights before you go to the ′Flower ″Show.

24 ⑤ 子音與子音的連接（記號：⌢ ）

前面我們看過子音與母音、母音與母音、母音與子音的連接，這些連
接使意群說起來流暢無阻。但子音與子音的連接却有不同的效果。做下面
的練習，注意子音和子音是如何連接起來的。

相同子音連接的練習

p- p

You must sto**p** **p**laying.

He won to**p** **p**lace.

It's a dee**p** **p**ool.

b- b

To ru**b** **b**oth eyes;

The ca**b** **b**roke down.

A great hu**b**-**b**ub;

t- t

I wen**t** **t**o town.

She a**t**(e) **t**en cookies.

We pu**t** **t**wo in the box.

d- d

He ha**d** **d**one it.

I saw a ma**d** **d**og.

They coul**d** **d**rive it.

c - c

A comic cartoon ;

Our music club ;

A public career ;

g - g

We saw the big game.

My bag got lost.

Did your egg get cold ?

j - j

A large jewel ;

I took orange juice.

In the village jail ;

m - m

It was the sam(e) man.

He becam(e) more at home.

He cam(e) many times.

r - r

Some paper roses ;

I never read.

Doesn't it ever rain ?

v - v

They hav(e) very good food.

We lov(e) vegetables.

We drov(e) very slowly.

k - k

He held a black king.

A sick kangaroo ;

They mak(e) kodaks.

f - f

Take off four pounds.

We're off for New York.

We'd laugh for an hour.

l - l

They all look alike.

Call Long Distance.

They sell little dolls.

n - n

They worked ten nights.

He can never do it.

That's his pen name.

s - s

Let's send a telegram.

It makes some sense.

They pass some cakes.

w - w

You can learn new ways.

A few women came.

A new washing machine.

y - y

　　The day you came.

　　The way you dress.

　　He'll buy your car.

sh - sh

　　Does she wash shirts ?

　　I wish she would come.

　　They're on the dish shelf.

th - th

　　They both thought about it.

　　With thanks.

z - z

　　He lost his zither.

　　The city was zoned.

　　The zoo has zebras.

ch - ch

　　He has a gold watch chain.

　　Speak to each child.

　　A rich Chinese merchant.

　　　　　　　　　　　　　　He's worth thousands.

不同的子音連接的練習，包括一個或更多個子音和下個字首的子音相連接：

　　　　一個子音　記號 - -

　　　　或三個以上子音　記號 ─ -

　　　　　　　　　　　　　　　二個子音　記號 ─ -

1. b─

　　He had a rub down.

　　A tulip bulb grower.

　　A barbed wire fence ;

2. c─

　　The civic center ;

　　Zinc bends easily.

　　Zinc's very soft.

3. d─

　　His grad(e) book ;

　　The grand stand ;

　　The band's playing.

4. f─

　　He got off the bus.

　　They played soft ball.

　　The twelfth time.

5. g —

I beg your pardon.

He never begs my pardon.

He begged her pardon.

g —

Don't judge me.

Fresh orange juice.

I arranged them.

6. k —

Do you lik(e) my wife ?

She likes good wine.

He links consonants.

7. l —

Call me at six thirty.

The bell's ringing.

He halts suddenly.

8. m —

Do you dream much ?

He dreams very often.

He warmed his hands.

9. n —

Six main points ;

It rains too much.

Against those ideas ;

10. p —

We hop(e) so.

We hoped so.

He stamped the letter.

11. r —

Far from home ;

The cars came at nine.

I warned them.

12. s —

I miss my parents.

She missed the train.

She rinsed the towels.

s —

Two ways to do it ;

He reads two hours.

He spends too much.

13. t —

He got sick.

They won't stay.

He wants to study.

14. v —

We've talked enough.

Their wives left.

He carved the turkey.

15. w —

They saw wood.

I sawed the wood.

She browned the bacon.

16. x —

The tax law ;

We waxed the floors.

A jinxed trip.

17. z —

His jazz band ;

A jazzed waltz ;

A cleansed conscience ;

18. ng —

Some sang songs.

They hanged him.

19. ch —

Two rich bankers ;

In march time ;

He wrenched his arm.

20. sh —

Some fresh flowers ;

The Welsh people ;

He welshed three times.

21. th —

They both think so.

It's worth trying.

Five twelfths stronger ;

th —

They breath(e) hard.

He breathed deeply.

She breathes more easily.

≈《Coffee Break》≈

If *W*ashington's *w*ife *w*ent to *W*ashington *w*hile *W*ashington's *w*ash*w*oman *w*ashed *W*ashington's *w*oolies, how many W's would there be in all ?

→ *There are no W's in " all ".*

　　如果當華盛頓的洗衣婦洗華盛頓的毛線衣時，華盛頓的太太到華盛頓去，共有多少個w？

→ " all " 裏沒有w。

✦這則看起來很順口，多唸幾次，會覺得越唸越有趣味。

　　in all " 總共 "

≈《Coffee Break》≈

What is the five-syllable word of which, if you take away one syllable, no syllable remains ?

→ *Monosyllable.*

　　哪個五音節的字，如果你拿掉一個音節，就沒一個音節剩下？

→ Monosyllable（單音節字）。

✦monosyllable 拿掉一個音節 mo，就留下 *nosyllable*，豈不是變成「沒有音節」！

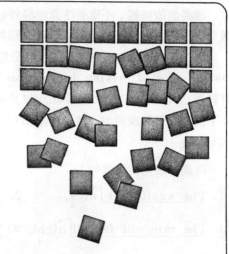

LESSON 25

本課旨在簡介英語的語調。一個句子以不同的語調說，代表不同的情緒，所以意思也有不同。了解語調變化的原則，能增加表達的效果。

25 ① 語調

　　說英語的時候，不僅要注意意群停頓、連音，還要注意到抑揚頓挫的效果，即語調與重音。這課將簡單介紹英語的語調，並做練習。

　　我們常將整個句子各段落的高低分爲五種，即平調（level intonation），昇調（rising intonation），降調（falling intonation），昇降調（rise-fall intonation）以及降昇調（fall-rise intonation）。在下列的介紹與練習中，將以線標出句子的語調昇降。

(a) 降調

　　降調一般用在直述句：

1. The weather is nice.　　2. The movie was good.

3. The rain will fall all night.　4. They said we were early.

5. My brother has a headache.　6. Your father had a briefcase.

7. She was wearing a red sweater.

8. You can finish the next lesson.

　　以 W 起首或 How 起首的疑問句：

1. When are you leaving ?

2. Why did you do it ?

3. What is your name ?

4. How do you like this picture ?

5. How old are you ?

6. What is the matter with you ?

7. When did you see it ?

8. What are you doing ?

命令句：

1. Bring me a pen.　　　　2. Open the door.

3. Shut the window.　　　　4. Bring me a cake.

(b) 昇調

昇調一般用在以 yes, no 回答的疑問句：

1. Do you speak English ?　　2. Do you have any brothers ?

3. Are you sure ?　　　　　4. Can you drive a car ?

5. Did he finish his work ?　　6. Is that your pencil ?

附加問句：

1. You want to read this story, don't you ?

2. He speaks German, doesn't he ?

3. He likes English, doesn't he ?

4. You are a student, aren't you ?

表懷疑、未定、猜測或期待等：

1. I think so.　　　　　2. She might have gone.

3. I thought it was right.　　4. She might have come.

表催促，或交待等：

1. Be early !　　　　　2. Don't be so angry.

3. Don't keep Mother waiting.

4. Come along.　　　　5. Don't be so foolish.

（c）**先昇後降**

如：1. one, two, three, four, five.

　2. He went, but she didn't.

　3. The seasons of the year are spring, summer, autumn, and winter.

　4. Is this a pen or a pencil?

　5. Do you want tea or coffee?

　6. Do you like water or juice?

25 ② 下面的句子標有語調，請跟著讀：

1. Bill can write, but he can't spell.

2. I ate food, but I wasn't hungry.

3. I made an appointment, but I didn't keep it.

4. The reason for the delay wasn't given.

5. How do you do, Mr. Wilson?

6. Good-bye, Dr. Nelson.

7. When are you leaving, Bill?

8. Why did you do it, Henry?

9. What is your name, little boy?

10. It was a good book, and I enjoyed it.

再做以下的練習：

Good morning,

| Bill. |
| Jane. |
| Mr. White. |
| Miss　Brown. |
| Dr. Brown. |
| Miss　Chen. |

25 ③ 以下是**疑問句的練習**，請跟著讀：

1. Are you here, Mary ?

2. Have you forgotten, Miss White ?

3. Are you going ?

4. Were they leaving ?

5. Did you do it ?

6. Did you understand Bob ?

7. Did you understand, Bob ?

8. Are you going to write John ?

9. Are you going to write, John ?

10. Did you call June ?

25 ④ 昇降調的練習

1. I'd like some bacon, eggs, and toast.

2. All she does is sleep, eat and play.

3. Mary was hungry, sleepy, and tired.

4. They have a lot of pens, pencils and hats.

5. Do you want to ride or walk?

6. Would you like coffee or tea?

7. Was he happy or sad?

8. Is it sunny or cloudy?

9. Would you like milk, tea, or coffee?

10. Do you want bread, milk, or butter?

學習出版，天天進步

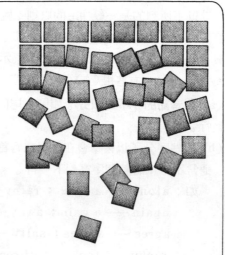

LESSON 26

本課介紹英文字分音節的一般規則。
分音節是打字時最需要的一項常識，
有時書寫也會用到。英文字拆寫分音
節有特殊的方式，與一般發音分音節
的情形不太一樣。

26 ① 音節的分法

以下所列的是一般採用的原則，雖然有些例外，但能幫助我們決定，寫的時候應該如何將行尾的字分音節。但最好是手邊有比較可靠的原文字典，可供隨時查閱。字典上音節的標示符號不只一種，如：syl̍la·ble，syl·la·ble。有些用（ˊ），有些用（·）。

（a）**單音節的字不可以分**。如果行尾的空間不夠寫，就將這個字寫在下一行。

（b）有些字分了以後，會在行尾或行首留下只有一個字母的字尾或字首，通常不分，將整個字寫到下一行。

> 如：alone —— a lone ; rainy —— rain y
>
> again —— a gain ; away —— a way
>
> agree —— a gree ; salty —— salt y
>
> rocky —— rock y ; abroad —— a broad

（c）多音節的字可在**字根**與**字首**（ prefix ）或**字尾**間分。

> 如：undone —— un done ; hopeful —— hope ful
>
> replacement —— re place ment ; movement —— move ment
>
> kindly —— kind ly ; useless —— use less
>
> friendship —— friend ship ; joyous —— joy ous

（d）多音節的字可在後面接有字尾（ suffix ）的重覆子音後分。

> 如：telling —— tell ing ; passing —— pass ing
>
> successful —— suc cess ful

（e）多音節的字可在不同的子音間分，二個子音共同發一個音時除外。

> 如：basket —— bas ket ; rapture —— rap ture
>
> handsome —— hand some ; friendship —— friend ship
>
> goodness —— good ness ; kindness —— kind ness
>
> conduct —— con duct ; 但是 chicken —— chick en

（f）多音節的字可在母音與子音間分，以便在每個音節中留一個母音。

如：table —— ta ble ； probably —— prob a bly

canoe —— ca noe ； cabin —— cab in

nation —— na tion ； civil —— civ il

(g) 多音節的字可在重覆的子音間分。

如：rabbit —— rab bit ； little —— lit tle

sufficient —— suf fi cient ； submissive —— sub mis sive

aggressive —— ag gres sive； occasion —— oc ca sion

(h) 多音節的字可在二個母音間分，但二個母音共同發一個音時除外。

如：create —— cre ate ； lion —— li on

但是 people —— peo ple

(i) **複合字**可按組成要素分。

如：playground —— play ground ； classmate —— class mate

railway —— rail way ； blackboard —— black board

||||||||||||| ● 學習出版公司門市部 ● |||||||||||||||||

台北地區：台北市許昌街 10 號 2 樓 TEL：(02)2331-4060・2331-9209
台中地區：台中市綠川東街 32 號 8 樓 23 室
　　　　　TEL：(04)2223-2838

|||||||||||||||||||||||||||||||||||||||||||||||||||||||

KK 音標發音秘訣

編　　著 ／ 吳 姍 姍
發 行 所 ／ 學習出版有限公司　　　　☎ (02) 2704-5525
郵 撥 帳 號 ／ 0512727-2 學習出版社帳戶
登 記 證 ／ 局版台業 *2179* 號
印 刷 所 ／ 裕強彩色印刷有限公司
台 北 門 市 ／ 台北市許昌街 10 號 2 F　　　☎ (02) 2331-4060・2331-9209
台 中 門 市 ／ 台中市綠川東街 32 號 8 F 23 室　　☎ (04) 2223-2838
台灣總經銷 ／ 紅螞蟻圖書有限公司　　　☎ (02) 2799-9490・2657-0132
美國總經銷 ／ Evergreen Book Store　　☎ (818) 2813622

售價：新台幣一百五十元正
2001 年 11 月 1 日一版八刷

ISBN 957-519-148-X